the nativity story

Tyndale House Publishers, Inc.
Carol Stream, Illinois

the nativity story

One family. One journey.
One child who would change the world forever.

A NOVELIZATION BY BEST-SELLING AUTHOR
ANGELA HUNT

BASED ON THE MOTION PICTURE WRITTEN BY
MIKE RICH

Visit Tyndale's exciting Web site at www.tyndale.com

TYNDALE and Tyndale's quill logo are registered trademarks of Tyndale House Publishers, Inc.

The Nativity Story: A Novelization

Copyright © MMVI New Line Productions, Inc. All rights reserved.

The Nativity Story: the novel by Angela Hunt from the screenplay by Mike Rich for the motion picture: based on the biblical narrative.

Photographs by Jaimie Trueblood. All photographs copyright © MMVI New Line Productions, Inc. All rights reserved.

Designed by Jacqueline L. Noe

Edited by Lorie Popp, Sarah Mason, and Jan Pigott

Scripture quotations are taken from the *Holy Bible*, New Living Translation, copyright © 1996. Used by permission of Tyndale House Publishers, Inc., Carol Stream, Illinois 60188. All rights reserved.

Some Scripture quotations are taken from the *Complete Jewish Bible*, copyright © 1998 by David H. Stern. Published by Jewish New Testament Publications, Inc. www.messianicjewish.net/jntp. Distributed by Messianic Jewish Resources, www.messianicjewish.net. All rights reserved. Used by permission.

Library of Congress Cataloging-in-Publication Data

Hunt, Angela Elwell, date.
    The nativity story / Angela Hunt ; developed from the screenplay by Mike Rich.
      p. cm.
    ISBN-13: 978-1-4143-1462-4 (pbk.)
    ISBN-10: 1-4143-1462-0 (pbk.)
    1. Jesus Christ—Nativity—Fiction. 2. Bible. N.T.—History of Biblical events—Fiction.
I. Rich, Mike, date. II. Title.
    PS3558.U46747N38 2006
    813'.54—dc22   2006026323

Printed in the United States of America

12	11	10	09	08	07	06
7	6	5	4	3	2	1

LOOK!

The virgin will conceive a child!

She will give birth to a son

and will call him Immanuel—

'GOD WITH US.'

ISAIAH 7:14

prologue

With one hand on her hip, Lavinia Dressler inhaled a deep breath and surveyed the spreading chaos. Two of the three wise men were pounding out "Heart and Soul" on the grand piano while one of the shepherds attempted to tie the belt of his bathrobe to the cow's tail. The two halves of the cow, a freckle-faced ten-year-old and her equally speckled brother, shoved and pushed, refusing to stand near each other, while the lamb kept wailing that her costume made her nose itch.

Lavinia blinked at the commotion. Whatever had made her think she could pull this off with only one dress rehearsal?

She clapped for her cast's attention, then nodded at a watching parent—Arlene Jessup, if memory served, mother to the wise man who kept trying to tickle Joseph's neck with straw. "Can you help me establish order in here?"

Arlene rose from the front pew and snapped her fingers in her son's direction. A couple of other parents followed Arlene's example and waded into the confusion, pulling characters, animals, and angels into position.

Turmoil, Lavinia reminded herself, was the risk one took when working with children and animals . . . and probably why she had neither children nor animals of her own.

"All right." She forced a smile as a headache began to tap on her temple. "When Mary and Joseph kneel by the manger, the rest of you will come in humming 'Silent Night.' Once everyone is standing in the proper spot, we'll sing. Everybody clear on that?"

She glanced at the three magi, who shuffled in the straw next to a band of bathrobed shepherds. Tommy Andrews, the tallest of the wise boys, lifted the lid off his mother's crystal candy dish and sniffed.

"Tommy? Do you have something in your bowl?"

The grinning boy tilted the contents in her direction. "Want a Jelly Belly?"

"No, thank you. And I'm sure the wise men didn't bring candy to the baby Jesus, so let's lose the jellies before tomorrow night, okay? Parents? Can we make sure the wise men aren't carrying any surprises?"

Arlene and the other adults nodded.

"Good." Lavinia clasped her hands and gave the young thespians her brightest smile. "As you sing, children, I want you to look at the baby Jesus. Mary, I want you to hold on to the baby as if he's the most important thing in the world. Can you do that for me?"

Jessica Harper, who'd been chosen to play the virgin, nodded, her blue eyes glowing. She tucked a strand of golden hair behind her ear, then clutched the doll to her chest as if he were the last available sweater at a Nordstrom's 90-percent-off sale.

Lavinia sighed. Jessica meant well, but she'd had no experience with babies. Joseph looked as if he'd rather be out skateboarding than standing beside an overstuffed manger, the magi knew more about Nintendo than stars, and though the shepherds could operate a computer, they couldn't find their way to the restroom and back without trailing straw down every hallway in the church.

But though her young actors may have lacked life experience, they knew this Christmas pageant. The holiday play had become a tradition at their small church; every year the pastor awarded the leading roles on the first Sunday after Thanksgiving. Christopher Stock, playing Joseph, had memorized the most Bible verses at middle school camp, and everyone quietly acknowledged Jessica Harper as the congregation's prettiest fourteen-year-old.

"All right now. Everyone stand perfectly still." Lavinia held up her hands, framed the stage between her extended forefingers and thumbs, and for a moment was struck speechless at the charming tableau: baby, manger, Mary, Joseph, shepherds, magi, animals, and angels, all fresh faced, scrubbed clean, and ready to smile for the camcorders.

How had the story become so . . . attractive?

She lowered her hands as a more realistic image supplanted the artfully arranged actors: a reeking animal pen in the dark of night, crowded by livestock and rats. . . .

"Children." The cast stopped fidgeting as Lavinia sank onto the stool in the center aisle. She took a moment to gather her thoughts, then looked out over the sea of immature faces. "I'm so glad you're willing to be a part of our Nativity play. You know your lines; you know the story. Some of you have seen this drama a dozen times."

Her gaze fell upon the blank-eyed doll in Jessica's pale arms. "But our Christmas pageant tells only a small part of what happened in Bethlehem. Mary and Joseph had experienced fear and exhaustion by the time they arrived in the city. The shepherds were the *last* people anyone expected to receive an invitation to visit the newborn baby, and the wise men traveled many dangerous miles to find the infant king."

Lavinia shuddered, imagining the perils of a first-century journey through untamed desert territory. Then she lifted her gaze to find Mikey Jessup watching her. The pint-sized wise man's eyes had gone as round as globes.

What was she *thinking*? These children were too young to hear about the terrors of travel and bloodthirsty tyrants. They didn't need to learn about shame and scandal and oppression—not yet.

Never mind that the virgin mother had been about Jessica's age when everything happened.

Lavinia shook off her thoughts, slipped from the stool, and lifted her hands. "On the last verse of 'Silent Night,' you wise men exit toward the piano, remember? Shepherds and animals, you follow them. Angels, hover around the baby Jesus until the music stops."

As their pure, youthful voices rang among the rafters, Lavinia shivered in another moment of vivid imagination. All was not calm on that long-ago evening in Bethlehem; all was not bright. For desperation shadowed the hearts of men, and evil fully intended to blot out the light.

chapter one

At the sound of voices, Mary pulled a square of linen over her hair, then scooped up the other three pieces of cloth and sprinted across the furrowed ground. All four girls had left their veils on a rock by the side of the road, certain they would be reaping alone in their families' fields. They had been left to themselves for most of the morning, but now the sun stood high overhead, and the voices that had reached Mary's ear belonged to *men*.

"Naomi!" she hissed, cupping her hand to her mouth. "Rebecca, Aliyah! Someone comes!"

The other girls, who had been laughing and calling to one another as they cut the tender heads of barley from the stalks, stopped and turned.

"Who comes?" Naomi wanted to know.

"I'm not sure," Mary said, tossing a rectangular cloth to her, "but they're men."

Rebecca and Aliyah left their rows and hastened to smooth their veils over their tumbling tresses.

With her back to the road, Mary felt for the edges of her own rough veil, then tucked a rebellious hank of hair behind her ear. No virtuous young woman would dare be so immodest as to publicly approach a man with her hair exposed, but each of the four friends had only recently entered womanhood. The habits of freewheeling childhood clung to them like vines.

Rebecca smoothed her veil and wiped a trickle of perspiration from her forehead. "How do I look?"

"You'll look better without seeds on your brow." Mary reached up to wipe a speckling of barley from Rebecca's damp forehead, then nodded. "You look fine."

"I only hope whoever it is deserves the trouble we're taking," Naomi groused, repositioning the leather strap of the bag on her shoulder. "If it's Josiah and his friends . . ."

Mary suppressed a smile as the girls moved toward the road. Naomi always made a fuss when Josiah came into view, and Mary suspected that Naomi complained far more than necessary. Surely it wasn't natural to spend so much time thinking about a boy unless you liked him more than a little.

Her thoughts scattered as a knot of young men crested the hill, Josiah among them. Mary saw Naomi blush when he looked her way.

"Greetings," Rebecca called to the group. "Come you to the fields to work or to play?"

"To work, of course." Josiah scowled in Naomi's direction. "As long as you girls don't get in our way."

Naomi stepped forward, her eyes blazing above a demure smile. "I do believe the four of us can work faster than the—" she paused to count—"six of you."

Josiah's scowl deepened. "Tend to your family's plot, woman. Your father sent me out here to keep an eye on you."

Naomi placed a hand on her hip as her lower lip edged forward in a pout. "And what business have you with my father? I can't believe he would speak to you, let alone permit you through our courtyard gate."

"He speaks to me often." Josiah left the other boys to step closer. "And he groans and moans most piteously because he has a headstrong daughter, one who will almost certainly never be married—"

"I will be married but certainly not to the likes of you!" Naomi's words would have stung if not for the smile on her lips and the challenge in her eyes.

Mary stood back, watching in amused wonder as Naomi took off across the field, barley spilling from her bag with every step.

Not willing to be dismissed, Josiah took off after her, catching the girl before they had run half the length of the field.

"I've seen her run faster," Rebecca whispered.

Mary laughed, and something stirred in her heart as Josiah caught Naomi by the waist and pulled her down.

"Should we . . . help her?" Aliyah asked, her voice small.

Mary kept her eye on the pair but shook her head. "They are only playing."

Rebecca turned, a look of wonder in her dark eyes. "Do you think he's really been talking to her father?"

Mary watched as Naomi and Josiah smiled at each other; then she shifted her gaze to the older boys, most of whom had already waded into their families' fields. "I think our fathers have begun to talk a lot about the future. We have begun our monthly courses, so we are old enough to make our fathers anxious about finding us husbands . . . and providing a dowry."

The three girls stood in silence under the cloud-heavy expanse of sky. Then Rebecca whispered what Mary had been thinking: "Sometimes I wish I could remain a child forever."

chapter two

With sure and steady fingers, Gaspar peeled the leather wrapping from the clay tablet and peered at the cuneiform writing.

"Are the words too faint?" Melchior asked, leaning over the edge of the table.

Gaspar's lips puckered with annoyance as he continued to squint at the tablet.

Aware of his student's irritation, Melchior settled his aging spine against the back of his chair and forced himself to exercise patience. Late-afternoon sunlight streamed through the open window and spangled the stone floor and tapestried walls. Across the chamber, on another table, a water clock revealed the passing of time, yet another reminder that each man had been given a finite number of hours to spend in the pursuit of knowledge.

Yearning to do something with his hands, Melchior picked up a scroll and blew the dust from it, then watched as the tiny particles rose in a column of shimmering light. "Think, Gaspar," he urged. "Does any of it apply? Any clue we find may be the final piece."

Gaspar exhaled an exasperated breath through his teeth and thrust the clay tablet away. "This is nothing but foolishness."

"This is discovery!" Melchior countered. "The words of the prophets have been proven true too many times for me to ignore them."

Gaspar gave him a black look, but Melchior had seen too many of

Gaspar's frowns to be offended. He tucked his hands into the sleeves of his robe and tipped his face toward the sun. "Please, tell me what you were reading. You know my eyes are not what they once were."

Gaspar sighed, then drew the tablet toward him again. " 'I see him,' " he translated, his voice slow and deliberate, " 'but not in the present time. I perceive him, but far in the distant future. A star will rise from Jacob; a scepter will emerge—' "

"From Israel?"

Gaspar lifted his gaze. " 'From Israel.' But, Melchior, surely this is not what you think. This is the prophecy of Balaam, son of Beor, and he was no son of Israel. How can we trust anything he would say about the Hebrews?"

Melchior closed his eyes. "How does a wise man know anything? Men know what the true God reveals, and God has revealed his truth—" he opened his eyes and spread his hand toward the window, indicating the room as well as the world beyond—"in his created order. In everything."

Not waiting for a reply, Melchior pushed himself up from his chair and passed into Balthasar's study. The younger man, who had made a specialty of astronomy, sat at a table cluttered by manuscripts, scrolls, and star charts. Two astrolabes and an armillary sphere weighted down several curled and yellowed papyri.

Balthasar, who had doubtless heard every word of the exchange in the room beyond, picked up the armillary sphere and turned the circles on their axes. " 'A star will rise from Jacob,' " he said, using his thumbs and forefingers to maneuver the zodiac and colures above the lumpy gem representing the earth, "but a star could represent any noteworthy person. So the prophet goes on to clarify—'a *scepter* will emerge from Israel.' And a scepter could only mean—"

"A king," Melchior finished.

Balthasar lowered the sphere. "Quite a king, if the rest of the prophecy is to be trusted. A king who will subdue all of Israel's enemies."

Though Gaspar continued to mumble in the distance, Melchior clasped his hands and sniffed with satisfaction. "I thought as much."

"Besides—" Balthasar's attention drifted back to the sphere on the table—"the prophet's words speak to a particular pattern I've been watching. Jupiter has tonight conjoined with Venus in the constellation of the Lion . . . so some important royal event is about to happen among the Jews."

Melchior crossed his arms. "If what Belteshazzar wrote is true, the Hebrew Messiah could come within our lifetimes. Perhaps this is what his God is revealing through the stars."

The mention of the ancient sage quieted Gaspar's muttering, as Melchior had known it would. Generations before, Belteshazzar, a Hebrew known to his people as Daniel, had mastered the wisdom and learning of the Chaldeans, surpassing even his teachers in knowledge and understanding. He attributed his wisdom to the one true God, an acknowledgment that puzzled some counselors of the royal court while it frustrated others. But Belteshazzar had so impressed the king of Babylon that he had been declared *rab-mag*, chief of all the wise men.

None of the chiefs who followed, not even Melchior, had deciphered or thoroughly explained the mysteries of Belteshazzar's prophetic writings.

But Melchior had not stopped trying.

"Esteemed teacher—" Gaspar stepped into the smaller chamber—"you must set aside this obsession with Belteshazzar. His words are a mystery, yes, but perhaps they are not meant to be understood."

"If they were not meant to be understood, why would Belteshazzar have written them? He was not one to waste words."

"If he wanted us to understand, why didn't he say what he meant? The man spoke in riddles."

"He spoke in code—and any code can be unlocked if a man has the required keys." Melchior closed his eyes in concentration. "'A period of seventy sets of seven has been decreed—'" he quoted the ancient prophecy from memory—"'for your people and your holy city to put down rebellion, to bring an end to sin, to atone for guilt, to bring in everlasting righteousness, to confirm the prophetic vision, and to anoint the Most Holy Place. Now listen and understand! Seven sets of seven plus sixty-two sets of seven will pass from the time the command is given to rebuild Jerusalem until the Anointed One comes.'"

To his left, he heard the sound of Gaspar pouring a cup of wine.

"Belteshazzar wrote of God's plan for his chosen people," Melchior continued, "and the Hebrews have long influenced the lands and people of the civilized world. The rab-mag wrote of seventy sevens, sixty-two sevens, and seven sevens. I have determined that the sevens are years, but the rest of the prophecy still baffles me."

Gaspar stepped into Melchior's field of vision and lifted his cup in a wry salute. "Nothing baffles you for long, my friend. You will either solve the riddle or drive us mad with your conjectures."

The old man glanced at his cynical protégé, then nodded at Balthasar. "You have long been interested in the Hebrews. Perhaps you can come up with an answer in Belteshazzar's text."

Balthasar picked up another faded scroll and ran his ink-stained fingertip along a line of script, his lips moving as he silently read the words. When he had finished, he lowered the scroll and shifted on his stool.

"In one sense," he said, speaking in his careful and deliberate way, "the meaning of the rab-mag's foretelling is obvious, for Artaxerxes issued a decree for the rebuilding of Jerusalem in the twentieth year of his reign. The Hebrews completed the rebuilding of Jerusalem forty-nine years after the decree was given; hence, Belteshazzar's first 'seven sets of seven' has been fulfilled. Sixty-two *additional* sevens must pass before their Messiah will be revealed, but only four hundred forty-nine years have passed since Artaxerxes' edict."

Melchior folded his hands. "Go on."

"So . . . if Belteshazzar's words can be trusted, within thirty-four years the Hebrews' anointed leader will arrive."

"Excellent calculations." Melchior nodded at his student. "But you have neglected to keep reading. Listen, if you will." He picked up the ancient scroll and squinted, forcing his aging eyes to focus on the familiar text. "'After this period of sixty-two sets of seven, the Anointed One will be killed, appearing to have accomplished nothing.'"

He lowered the scroll and cocked a brow at Balthasar. "The appointed time refers to the *death* of the Anointed One, not his arrival."

"Bah." Gaspar lowered his cup to the table. "The first prophecy speaks of a king who will subdue Israel's enemies. How can *this* king, if Belteshazzar wrote of the same man, be killed before he accomplishes anything? Impossible."

Balthasar shrugged. "There are too many unknowns for us to make an exact calculation. A man may die at any age, so how can we know when he will be born? We would need a reference point, something solid."

Melchior stroked his beard, then shifted his gaze to the armillary sphere. "We have a reference point. The heavens."

From the corner of his eye, Melchior saw Gaspar shake his head, but Balthasar picked up the armillary sphere and began to manipulate the rings. "Why shouldn't Belteshazzar's invisible God leave messages in the natural order of his universe? For instance, if Venus and Jupiter draw near each other in the skies above Jerusalem . . ."

He moved the band going around the sphere, the ring representing the zodiac, then stopped. By the slight squint of his eye and sideways movement of his jaw, Melchior knew the younger astronomer had arrived at a conclusion. "In how many years should we expect a king?"

Balthasar gave his mentor a bright-eyed glance. "It will not be years, my esteemed friend."

chapter three

"'Hear, O Isra'el! The Lord is our God, ADONAI alone. . . .'"

Zechariah closed his eyes as the leader continued the morning prayers and called the faithful to worship. For over forty years he had made the pilgrimage from Juttah to Jerusalem so that he might serve his course of service in the Temple. Now, in the autumn of his life, his spirit had wearied of the journey.

He and his wife, Elizabeth, had lived blameless lives before God and man, observing the *mitzvot* and ordinances of ADONAI, and for what? He had never been chosen to serve in the Holy Place.

Elizabeth had never been blessed with a child.

Despite their many prayers, despite their devotion to ADONAI and the Law, Zechariah and his wife would die poor and childless. His neighbors called him doubly blessed, for he was a *cohen* from the order of Abijah and Elizabeth had descended from the priestly order of Aaron. But of what use was a godly heritage if a man could not bequeath it to sons and daughters?

The prayers concluded, and those who had previously offered incense discreetly backed away. Zechariah looked around, realizing with a pang that he was the oldest man remaining in the circle. Like a virgin daughter for whom no man asks, he stood with the younger priests and waited, once again, for the Spirit of ADONAI to move in the casting of lots and pass him by.

His heart thumped against his rib cage when the leader motioned for him to remove his head covering. He obeyed, feeling gray and vulnerable, and lifted his hand with the others. Since the Law forbade the counting of persons, the leader would begin with the bareheaded priest and count fingers. Some men held up four fingers, others two or three. Because the offering of incense was the most sacred duty a priest could render, Zechariah felt a humble man should extend only one.

The leader had already counted off two lots. The first, which had occurred early in the morning, selected a priest to cleanse and prepare the altar. The second designated the priest who would approach the Holy Place to offer the sacrifice, trim the candlestick, and clear the altar.

The leader announced a number—seventy-one—and fingers fluttered and settled as he began counting again, moving swiftly around the circle of upraised hands.

Zechariah lowered his gaze, unwilling to watch. He had learned to soften disappointment by anticipating it, so in a moment he would back away, put on his headgear, and slip into the congregation, where he would pray with hundreds of other sons of Isra'el.

"Sixty-eight, sixty-nine, seventy . . . seventy-one."

Zechariah's throat went dry when the leader's bulky form filled his field of vision.

"You, Zechariah." Awe filled the leader's voice, not for the chosen *cohen* but out of respect for the honor. "HaShem, blessed be he, has chosen you to offer incense before the altar."

Zechariah nodded, not certain he could trust his voice to reply. More than fifty *cohanim* stood with him in the Hall of Hewn Polished Stones, yet *he* had been selected to perform this most important task. The privilege of offering the incense symbolizing Isra'el's accepted prayers could not be repeated in a man's lifetime.

Yet once was enough. After this day, Zechariah would be called *rich*, for the Torah promised blessing to the Levites who served God by offering incense.

With his work assigned, Zechariah stepped out of the circle, his thoughts centering on his task. "They will 'teach your regulations to Jacob,' " he murmured under his breath. " 'They will present incense before you and offer whole burnt offerings on the altar. Bless the Levites, O Lord, and accept all their work.'"

Soft ripples of congratulation reached his ear as the leader counted off the fourth lot, which would select a priest to place the sacrifice on the altar and pour out the drink offerings.

Zechariah had stood in the Hall of Hewn Stones more than eighty times, so he knew what to do. As soon as the leader finished the final count, Zechariah would choose two friends or relatives to assist in his sacred duty. One would clear the altar, removing everything that remained from the previous evening's service, and reverently leave the Holy Place by walking backward. The second assistant would step forward with a bowl containing live coals taken from the altar of the burnt offering. He would spread the coals to the edge of the golden altar, then walk backward from the Holy Place, leaving Zechariah alone to fulfill the responsibility God had given him.

Holding the golden censer, he would stand on bare feet in the soft light of the seven-armed candlestick. He would look toward the altar glowing with red-hot coals and situated before the heavy veil separating the Holy Place from the Holy of Holies. He would wait until he heard the worship leader proclaim that the time of incense had come; then he would step forward and place the incense on the altar, as near to the Holy of Holies as possible. Like the prayers of the people in the Temple beyond, a fragrant cloud would rise heavenward.

Zechariah would bow low in worship and reverently retreat as the people in the courtyard chanted, "Appoint peace, goodness, and blessing; grace, mercy, and compassion for us, and for all Isra'el. Bless us, O our Father, all of us as one, with the light of your countenance. For in the light of your countenance have you, Jehovah, our God, given us the Law of life, and loving mercy, and righteousness, and blessing, and compassion, and life. . . ."

When the prayers had been offered, Zechariah would turn at the top of the stairs. Every eye would be focused upon him as he lifted his hands in the traditional gesture and recited the benediction: *"Y'varekh'kha ADONAI v'yishmerekha."* May the Lord bless you and protect you.

"*Ya'er ADONAI panav eleikha vichunekka.*" May the Lord smile on you and be gracious to you.

"*Yissa ADONAI panav eleikha v'yasem l'kha shalom.*" May the Lord show you his favor and give you his peace.

Zechariah had to blink away tears as a priest from Jerusalem came toward him and dipped his chin in shallow acknowledgment. Zechariah and the others from his village knew what the Temple priests thought of them. The Levites from the hill country were not wealthy or learned. Most of them studied Torah in their village synagogues, not under the esteemed scholars who ran schools in Jerusalem. The Temple cohanim called them *Amha-arets*, rustic priests, and treated them with gentle disdain. Their service was tolerated, for they were descended from the tribe of Levi, but they were not welcomed.

Zechariah tucked his hands into the sleeves of his robe and addressed the Jerusalem priest. "I know what to do." He turned and nodded at his kinsman Uriah. An unspoken understanding passed between them as their gazes connected. "Will you, my brother, assist with clearing the altar?"

After being rewarded with an enthusiastic smile, Zechariah turned to Uriah's brother Nahshon, another cohen from the Judean town where Zechariah lived. "And will you assist with the coals?"

Nahshon bowed his head. "I would be honored."

Zechariah turned to the priest from Jerusalem. "I am ready."

With his two rustic assistants, Zechariah approached the altar of burnt offering. The muscles of his forearms hardened beneath his sleeves as he filled the golden censer with incense and his second assistant piled burning coals within the golden bowl. With the first assistant, they passed from the Court of the Priests and struck the *magrephah*, the sound of which called priests throughout the Temple to worship.

Conscious of the pressure of scores of eyes, Zechariah ascended the stairs to the Holy Place with slow and deliberate steps. The two priests who had been chosen to dress the altar and the candlestick went before him and withdrew the vessels they had left behind.

Zechariah lifted his gaze to the huge golden vine fastened above the double doors. The vine symbolized Isra'el, and the smallest cluster of grapes dangling from its stem dwarfed Zechariah's aging form. If HaShem, blessed be he, had wanted the vine to make his people feel small, he had certainly accomplished his purpose.

The blue, scarlet, and purple curtains over the doors to the Holy Place had been pulled back, the gold-plated doors exposed. Zechariah drew a deep breath, then nodded to his assistants and moved forward.

He waited before the altar, the hard fist of anxiety clenching in his stomach as his fellow priests performed their tasks. After so long, why had ADONAI chosen this day to honor his lifetime of service? Perhaps he should prepare to die . . . or perhaps ADONAI's reason shouldn't matter.

Elizabeth had to be thrilled to know that Zechariah had finally been chosen.

All the relatives would be pleased.

The assistants, their work complete, bowed and withdrew from the Holy Place, backing through the doorway and down the steps as carefully as they had approached.

Zechariah inhaled the sweet perfume of incense as he waited for the Levite worship leader's command. He lifted his gaze to heaven. While the worshippers outside this room offered the prescribed prayers, he couldn't help but add the habitual plea of his heart: *Jehovah my God, your name is from everlasting, and there is no God beside you. If it is possible I have pleased you, my King, once again may I beg you to grant my prayer for a son before I breathe my last—*

"The time of incense has come!"

Hearing the worship leader's cry above the shuffle of kneeling bodies, Zechariah urged his feet forward. He caught his breath as he spread the incense on the hot coals, then exhaled when a spiral of smoke rose into the still air of the sacred space. He whispered his prayers along with the leader as plumes of gentle white smoke swirled before him. . . .

Like the prayers of his people.

Like his prayers. And Elizabeth's.

He lowered the empty censer, preparing to bow and leave the

Holy Place, but something moved in the smoke, a wavering form that *should not be*.

"Zechariah."

A memory surfaced, unbidden. From where did the shekinah speak to Moses? From the altar of incense. But this could not be the voice of God, nor his form, for God had not spoken even through his prophets in years.

"Zechariah."

The voice, a roaring whisper, filled the space around the altar, yet Zechariah did not think anyone in the courtyard could hear it. The low rumble, at once powerful and gentle, *spoke his name*.

As terror blew down the back of his neck, Zechariah peered into the swirling smoke.

In the Court of the Women, the farthest point a female could venture into the Temple, Elizabeth lifted her hands and joined in the morning prayers. From the raised gallery that ran along three sides of the rectangular chamber, she could look down into the Temple and observe all the proceedings. . . .

Except the sacred rites reserved for the Holy Place.

At this moment, Zechariah, her beloved husband, stood in that chamber, an honor for which he had waited a lifetime. By now he had to be spreading the incense on the altar. Soon he would emerge, his lined and dignified face lit by joy.

They had not known an abundance of joy in their life together. Though they had both been born into the priestly line of Isra'el, neither Zechariah nor Elizabeth had achieved any noteworthy success among their people. Their parents had arranged their marriage, confident it would be a good match, and as Zechariah joyfully led Elizabeth to the wedding feast, her friends had waved palm branches and shouted, "May ADONAI make you as fruitful as Rachel and Leah!"

The marriage had been a good match, for they had found happiness and love with each other. Yet while Elizabeth had never had reason to find fault with her husband, she had occasionally suppressed the urge to find fault . . . with God.

She could barely hold such a thought in the sacred space of the Temple. She and her priest husband had given their lives in holy service. They did not live in the luxurious Ophel Quarter in Jerusalem, home to so many cohanim, or in prosperous Jericho. They had made a home in quiet Juttah, which Zechariah departed without complaint every time his service fell due.

As a young bride, Elizabeth had been content to trust in ADONAI. Confident that children would come in God's good time, she had helped establish a home filled with love, integrity, and reverence toward everything the Law held sacred. She worked hard to keep her house clean, she met her husband's needs, and both of them strove to maintain a tender heart and open hand for the poor. Elizabeth never saw a tear fall without imagining it on her own cheek, and her husband made a practice of looking for the image of ADONAI in every man.

And how had ADONAI repaid them? By keeping them from riches so they would not become proud. By giving them only their daily bread so they could not become gluttons. By withholding the sacrament of service in the Holy Place from Zechariah and, hardest to accept, by preventing Elizabeth from bearing children. Why had God granted them such severe mercies?

With every passing year, Elizabeth found it harder to imagine a satisfactory answer.

The village women gossiped about her barrenness. Some said her womb remained empty because her heart brimmed with pride; other tongue waggers declared that Zechariah must have committed some secret sin. And as the years passed and Elizabeth's neighbors' houses quaked with the commotion of children, she sat by her cook fire and wondered why HaShem, blessed be he, had chosen to bless her with food, shelter, and the love of a good man—everything *but* her heart's desire.

Through months and years of frustration, Elizabeth stilled her protests and struggled to accept the will of God. HaShem, blessed be his name, gave and took away. He uplifted one family and lowered another.

He decreed a time for war and a time for peace. He created the fruitful womb . . . and the barren.

Yet today, miracle of miracles, he had honored her husband. Elizabeth had seen Zechariah lead his Judean assistants up to the Holy Place; she had watched him walk through the golden doors.

After a lifetime of service, ADONAI had decided to honor their faithfulness.

Blessed be the name of the Lord.

Peering into the space at the right of the altar, Zechariah beheld what he could only suppose was an angelic form. The being appeared human, with arms, legs, a torso, and a head—but in the marrow of his bones Zechariah knew this was no mortal creature. The man spoke, but his words did not leave the chamber; he stood next to the burning coals, but his glowing skin did not pearl with perspiration.

The trembling priest choked back a cry.

"Don't be afraid, Zechariah," the being said, "for God has heard your prayer, and your wife, Elizabeth, will bear you a son. You are to name him John. You will have great joy and gladness, and many will rejoice with you at his birth, for he will be great in the eyes of the Lord."

Zechariah forced a smile over skin that was taut with terror.

The angel—surely that's what he was—smiled, his features suffusing with joy. "Your son must never touch wine or hard liquor, and he will be filled with the Holy Spirit even before his birth. He will persuade many Israelites to turn to the Lord their God." The angel took a half step closer and bent as if to look more closely at the quivering priest before him. "He will be a man with the spirit and power of Elijah, the prophet of old. He will precede the coming of the Lord, preparing the people for his arrival. He will turn the hearts of the fathers to their children, and he will change disobedient minds to accept godly wisdom."

Somehow, Zechariah found his tongue. "How—how can I know

this will happen? I'm an old man now, and my wife is also well along in years."

The angel straightened. His handsome face transformed, the compassionate veneer peeling back to reveal the power beneath. "I am Gabriel! I stand in the very presence of God, and he sent me to bring you this good news. Now, since you didn't believe what I said, you won't be able to speak until the child is born. For my words will certainly come true at the proper time."

Then, dissipating like the smoke of incense, the image of Gabriel, messenger of God, faded from view.

Without thinking, Zechariah reached for something to steady himself, then remembered where he was. He, a lump of mortal clay, did not dare touch anything in this holy place.

He crumpled to the floor, dropping the sacred censer, and clasped his bony shoulders. What had happened? He had prayed for a sign, he had received an answer, and how did he respond? He doubted!

HaShem, blessed be he, had promised Abraham a child, and Abraham did not doubt. Sarah had laughed, but Zechariah was more foolish than that old woman. He'd looked into the face of Gabriel and said, "How can this happen? I'm an old man."

He shook his head, dumbfounded by his own stupidity. He had been granted an opportunity to speak with the holy messenger who once appeared to Daniel, and what had he done? Stammered out doubts and excuses!

Zechariah pressed his hand to his face, blew out a long breath, and forced himself to stand on wobbly legs. He could not stay here. He'd already proven his unworthiness, but the waiting priests beyond would think he'd been struck dead if he did not come out soon.

Perhaps God would have mercy. Perhaps—if he did not faint or collapse on his way out of this sacred sanctuary—God would allow him a measure of grace and forgive his dullness of mind.

Zechariah picked up the empty censer, gathered his courage, and opened the golden door.

A sea of faces stared up at him, most of them marked by curiosity. He saw the same expression on his two assistants: *What took you so long?*

Zechariah moved to the top of the stairs, handed the censer to Uriah, and lifted his arms for the ceremonial benediction. He opened his mouth, drew a breath . . . and no sound came forth.

Not a word.

chapter four

Anna paused at the gate to her courtyard and drew her mantle closer around her shoulders before lifting the latch. The rising wind that blew from the sea was not cold, but her husband's disapproval could be.

Joaquim sat before the cook fire in the center of the room, his eyes distracted. "Did you find her?"

Anna pulled her veil from her head and hung it on a peg by the door. "She was in the fields. I sent her to deliver a cheese to Ruth's house."

Joaquim grunted. "I trust she will come home in good time. It will not look good if she's late because she had to stop and talk to everyone she meets."

Anna pulled a bag of lentils from her basket. "Some men would be pleased with a daughter who takes time to talk with others. Mary has a soft heart, especially for children."

"She can tend to children when she is married, with a family of her own. Now she should be thinking about a husband. She is of age, and you must resign yourself to letting her go . . . as must I."

Anna poured the lentils into her pot and felt the sting of tears. She turned her head, hoping Joaquim wouldn't see the gleam of wetness on her lashes, but he was too quick for her.

"Anna"—he gentled his voice—"don't you remember how happy you were when I came to your father's house for the first time?"

She dashed a tear away and in that moment decided to uncover a secret she'd buried for nearly twenty years. "I wasn't happy," she whispered, her gaze meeting his. "I was terrified. I scarcely knew you."

A flash of surprise shone in his eyes, followed by a moment's lingering hurt. "Did I . . . I mean, were you . . . disappointed?"

"No, Husband. I grew to love you."

"And in those first days of our marriage . . . you trusted your father, didn't you?"

"If I had not trusted him, I would not have gone with you."

Joaquim smiled and straightened his spine. "You see? Like a good daughter, Mary will trust me. She will be happy when I give her the news."

"You are her father." Anna kept her voice light but looked toward the darkening window so he wouldn't see that she couldn't stop her tears. Mary brought sunlight and joy into the house. Could anyone blame a mother for not wanting to lose her only child?

"Where," she asked, forcing words over the lump in her throat, "is your brother? He was supposed to bring a fish for my stewpot."

Joaquim mumbled something about Aaron taking his girls to visit the fish markets at Magdala, but Anna barely heard his reply.

After stirring the lentils into the stew, she moved to the small front window. The dark clouds had opened, and through sheets of rain she saw a veiled figure running through the street, a woman leading a child with each hand.

The woman slowed to deliberately splash through a puddle while the children shrieked in delight.

Smiling, Anna leaned against the sill and wiped her cheek with her fingertips. Mary. Ruth must have sent two of her young ones to greet Mary at the city gate. Now the rain had drenched all three.

Anna kept her eyes on her daughter as Mary passed the house where Jacob the carpenter and his sons were working under the shelter of a roof. The carpenter's oldest son paused as the rain-soaked trio passed, and something in his expression piqued Anna's curiosity. . . .

Her husband had not told her whom he had spoken to about their daughter's betrothal, but for the past several days he had visited the widowed silk merchant who operated a booth in the marketplace. Anna did not want to oppose her husband's decisions, but she would not like to see Mary married to a dour-faced merchant, no matter how wealthy the widower was.

The carpenter's son, however, had a kind face, and he had looked at Mary with something in his eyes. . . .

Anna could only hope her husband had been open-minded enough to visit Jacob's house.

chapter five

Safely sheltered in Ruth's home, Mary ran a piece of linen over the little boy's form, then gave his wet head a final scrub with her fingertips. "There," she said, releasing him. "Go stand by the fire and soon you'll be as crisp as a brown leaf."

Jubal grinned and scampered to his sister, who was holding her fingers above the glowing embers. Ruth, whose house practically bulged with offspring, sent Mary an appreciative smile as she settled her baby into his basket. "Thank you," she said, collapsing onto a small stool. "I wouldn't have sent them to meet you if I had known ADONAI was going to send another flood."

"I'm sorry I was late." Mary sank to the woven mat with Ruth's young ones. "Time slipped away out in the fields. The harvesting took longer than I thought it would."

Ruth's cheek curved in a smile as she sat next to the children. "I remember my days of harvesting barley. My friends and I would pretend to cut the grain while we watched the boys at work in their families' fields. It's a miracle we harvested anything in those days."

"We didn't only pretend to work . . . though we *did* notice the boys." Mary lowered her gaze, alarmed that she'd brought up what could be an embarrassing subject. Ruth might ask if Mary's father had begun to receive visits from fathers of suitable prospects; then Mary would have to confess that her father hadn't mentioned anything, perhaps because no one wanted *his* daughter.

Ruth sighed and dropped her hand to the top of her pregnant belly. "Sometimes I wish I could be your age again. Life seemed easier when I was young."

"Has life in Nazareth ever been easy?" Eager to change the subject, Mary clapped for the children's attention. "Would you like to hear a story?"

As the five older children chorused their excitement, Ruth cast Mary a look of gratitude and rose to prepare their dinner.

Mary pulled young Jubal onto her lap, then proceeded to tell the familiar story of Elijah's testing. "Elijah," she began, "was a great prophet."

"The greatest," Jubal added.

Mary tilted her head and smiled. "I don't know if he was *the* greatest, but he was great. Yet when Jezebel the wicked queen wanted to kill him, the prophet was terrified."

Though she'd heard the story at least a dozen times, Levana stood and pressed her hands to her round cheeks. "Was he *afraid* of the wicked *queen*?"

"Absolutely." Mary glanced out the window, where lightning crackled above the horizon. "But Elijah shouldn't have worried, because HaShem, blessed be he, sent an angel to take care of him. The angel touched the prophet and said, 'Get up and eat some more, for there is a long journey ahead of you.'"

"I've never been on a long journey," Sarah said, rising to her knees. "Have you?"

Mary touched the young girl's shoulder. "You've been to Jerusalem, right? Well, that's a long journey, but Elijah had to go even farther. So to prepare himself, the prophet ate and drank, and the food gave him enough strength to travel all the way to Mount Sinai, the mountain of God. For forty days he walked before he came to a cave in the mountain of God—"

Always fond of attention, Levana whirled to face the others. "I'd be scared. I don't like caves."

"Now, Levana." Mary tugged on the little girl's hair. "You wouldn't be afraid, not with ADONAI to take care of you. As Elijah stood in the cave, ADONAI passed by, and a mighty windstorm hit the mountain. The blast was so strong that the rocks tore loose—"

"But ADONAI was not in the wind," the children chorused.

Mary nodded her approval. "After the wind there came an earthquake—"

"But ADONAI was not in the earthquake."

"And after the earthquake there came a fire—"

"But ADONAI was not in the fire."

Mary lowered her voice. "And after the fire there came—"

The children mimicked her tone: "The sound of a gentle whisper."

She smiled around the circle of upturned faces. "You're so smart! When Elijah heard the whisper, he wrapped his face in his cloak and went out and stood at the entrance of the cave. That's when God told him what he had to do."

Ruth, stewpot in hand, stepped into the story circle. "And now your mother will tell you what to do—go wash your hands. When you have finished, come sit on your mats."

Mary helped young Jubal slip from her lap and watched him run to join his siblings at the pitcher and basin.

With the children occupied, Ruth knelt and accepted the wrapped cheese Mary had brought in her bag. "This looks wonderful. Thank your mother for me."

She pressed a coin into Mary's palm and pulled a wrapped loaf from a nearby basket. "I'd like you to accept this. It's good bread, if I can say so without seeming immodest."

"Ruth, you keep it. You need to feed your children."

"We have enough. Trade at the market has been steady." Ruth pushed the bread into Mary's lap, then rested her hand on the younger girl's arm. A faint line appeared between her brows. "I hate to ask, but I think I should."

"Ask what?"

"You understand I only want to know because I care about you,

Mary. I would never forgive myself if it lay within my power to help and I did nothing—"

"*What*, Ruth?"

The young woman's mouth clamped tight as she swallowed hard. "Herod's tax collectors will be here tomorrow. Does your father have enough to pay his tax?"

Mary's cheeks flushed against the cool air from the window. "He does not speak to me of such things."

"But this is a small village, and people talk. I know the crops have not yet come in. I pray that he's strong. Men have had their children taken to satisfy their debt—"

"My father would never allow that."

"Of course not. Of course he wouldn't."

Mary lifted her gaze and saw unspoken worry lingering in the young woman's eyes. Some poor families, unable to afford the payment of taxes to Rome and Herod, sold their daughters into slavery. In some cases the young women were sold as brides and awarded the rights of a wife, but in other situations they were subjected to slavery. Female slaves could not be sold to foreigners, but neither could they be freed at the end of six years as a male slave would be.

"My father," she stressed, "is a good man."

"I know." Ruth caught Mary's hand and squeezed it. "You are a good daughter. Have faith in ADONAI, blessed be he. Times will soon be better for all of us."

Mary nodded, not wanting to argue, but she couldn't stop the anxiety in Ruth's eyes from spilling into her own heart.

Mary lifted the edge of her robe and picked her way home through the mud. The rain had stopped, but the mire would remain until the next morning's sun rose to bake the earth again.

She loved the first hour after a rain. The air smelled clean, and the colors of Nazareth took on deep and radiant hues once the dust had been washed away. The feathery palms were greener, the oranges sweeter smelling, and the olive trees shimmered with more silver in their leaves.

She also loved her hometown. Though the family's pilgrimages to Jerusalem never failed to stir her, she would never want to live anywhere but on the sloping streets of Nazareth. Most of the homes were simple structures of clay brick, nothing like the glorious palaces she'd glimpsed in Jerusalem, but on the road back to Galilee, when her love for ADONAI and hope for the consolation of Isra'el crowded her heart, the sight of her little city nestled against the breast of Mount Tabor awakened within her a yearning to nestle against the breast of ADONAI himself.

She misjudged a step and slipped into a gully, landing on her hip with a solid thump. Grimacing, she glanced toward the nearby windows to see if any of her neighbors had seen her spill—apparently not. If they had, they'd have called to her . . . or laughed.

She checked her bundle to be sure the bread hadn't been ruined and noted with relief that the fabric wrapping remained intact. She pushed herself up from the street and turned to assess the stain on her tunic. This garment would need washing, along with her veil. Her father would chide her for her carelessness if he saw her like this, but her mother would remain silent. Only when she and Mary were alone would she smile and help Mary scrub the mud from the worn linen.

Mary brushed a twisted hank of hair from her brow and grimaced when she felt the grit of sand beneath her fingertips. Now she had streaked her face with mud too.

She sighed, grateful that the sudden downpour had cleared the streets. In a moment she would be home, away from prying eyes.

She pulled her veil lower and hurried down a narrow alley, turning at the walled courtyard outside their one-room house. The aroma of wet goat greeted her as she lifted the latch. When she stepped into the yard, two horned heads swiveled in her direction.

"No comments from you two," she whispered. She was about to hurry through the curtain that served as their door, but the sound of male voices stopped her cold. She hesitated outside the curtain, her free hand extended, a tide of gooseflesh rippling up each arm. These were not the voices of her father and uncle. So who had braved the rain to visit?

"Come in, Mary." *That* was her father's voice, and Mary felt her face heat as she stared at the tattered curtain. Behind her, the sun had come out, casting her shadow upon the linen—a dark silhouette that was certainly visible to anyone inside the house. Their guests, whoever they were, had to have seen her hesitation.

She lifted the curtain and stepped inside, then dropped the loaf of bread and stood in humble obedience before her father. Keenly aware of her muddy garments and face, she did not look at the three shadowed figures standing at her right.

"Mary." No emotion in her father's greeting, no welcome. Only resignation.

His reticence sent alarm bells clanging within her. She lifted her eyes. "Father? Has something happened to Uncle Aaron or one of the girls?" Her hand flew to her throat. "Is Grandfather Avram—?"

"He is well. Everyone is well."

"Then why—?"

"Be silent, Mary, and listen." His face, which usually wore a firm expression even on feast days, had gone as blank as a mask. "My daughter, every woman must, at some point, leave her father and mother. It is ADONAI's ordained plan."

She blinked, still not trusting herself to look at the other figures in the room. Behind her father, on a mat, her mother sat by her stewpot, silently stirring. To Mary's right, the unknown trio waited.

She bowed her head. "I know, Father."

"This is the carpenter Jacob. He has brought his sons Joseph and Shem."

She hesitated, then lifted her gaze to take in the strangers. The men who stood against the wall looked familiar; she had seen them working in town. Custom forbade her from speaking to any of them, of course, but they appeared pleasant enough. The younger son especially, since he was probably only a year or two older than Mary.

"Jacob," her father went on, "wishes to betroth you to his eldest son, Joseph. He has brought the *shitre erusin*, drawn up by the authorities, and everything is in order."

Despite the warmth of the house, Mary felt her stomach contract into a cold knot. She had known this day would come ever since she began her monthly courses. Some families arranged the betrothal of their daughters long before the girls reached the age of childbearing, but Mary had hoped she might remain with her parents for several more years.

She did not feel ready to marry. What did she know of men? of motherhood?

She shifted her gaze from the floor to the legs of the man she would soon call husband. His sandals were well made, his legs strong and sturdy. Pads of flesh marked his knees while dark hair covered his arms. His calloused hands were twice the width of hers, and with those arms he could probably carry a pair of girls her size.

Reluctantly, she examined his face. A brown beard, tinged with gold, a straight nose, and two brown eyes that softened when her gaze brushed them. Brackets around his mouth gave him a look of resolve, and he held his head high.

Like her father, this man would not be commanded by a woman.

Mary averted her eyes as blood began to pound in her temples. For an instant she felt a dart of jealousy for Naomi—she would be betrothed to Josiah, who would grow old with her. But this Joseph was a man full formed, with a deep voice and strong limbs. A man who would take her to live in his house and expect her to provide him with sons and daughters.

She drew herself up and swallowed to dislodge her heart from her throat. "Joseph."

He nodded when she whispered his name. "I have brought this," he said, pulling a square of fine wool from beneath his cloak, "as the *mohar*. Our fathers have agreed upon our mutual obligations and your dowry."

He hesitated, and for an instant Mary wondered if he could possibly be as nervous as she. She had her answer when she accepted his gift and felt a slight tremble in the hand beneath the white fabric square.

"I want you to know that I have done everything possible to protect you," he continued. "If something happens to me, you will not be left without property. I have brought the writings of betrothal, and I deliver them to you."

He extended the shitre erusin, which Mary also accepted. "It is written," Joseph said, obviously understanding that Mary could not read, "that I have promised not to make you leave the land of Isra'el, or the town of Nazareth, or exchange a good house for a bad house without your consent. Within a year, I will come for you and take you as my bride, according to the law of Moses and Isra'el. I promise to please, honor, nourish, and care for you, as is the manner of the men of Isra'el."

Not knowing what else to do, Mary nodded while her father took the parchment from her hand. While she watched, he unfolded it, then used a charred stick to sign the document. Joseph's father did the same, and the agreement became binding.

"Jacob and I are witnesses," her father said as he folded the contract. "You will remain with us another year before Joseph comes to take you to your marriage feast. But you shall consider him your husband in all manner except that which leads to children. On that, the Law is clear."

"Congratulations, my friend." Jacob slapped Mary's father on the back, then lifted a wineskin. "We must share a glass to seal the arrangement. Come, have your wife bring cups for us."

Mary stood without speaking as her father, Jacob, and Shem moved toward the cook fire, where her mother was setting out pottery cups. Yet Joseph remained, standing beside Mary with the solidity of a mountain.

She took a deep breath, knowing she should not be afraid of her future husband. "Joseph," she repeated, fitting the word to her tongue as she set his bridal gift on a shelf. "I . . . I have seen you in the village."

He nodded, eagerness mingling with tenderness in his eyes. "I will provide a good home for you, Mary. You have my word."

"You are . . . a carpenter?"

"It is a good living. We will not be rich, but we will be happy. I will build you a house, big enough for a family, and when it is ready I will come for you."

Mary smiled, not trusting her voice. How many times had she told the village children to trust ADONAI for their daily bread? Surely the Lord could be trusted for something as important as marriage. He had sent her a husband, a man called Joseph. Like his namesake, this man might also prove to be a wise provider in a time of crisis.

"Joseph, Mary!" Shem called from the center of the room and held out a cup. "Come and drink to your marriage!"

The carpenter's eldest son gave Mary a reluctant parting smile and moved toward the circle of men. Mary watched him go, then accepted the cup her mother placed in her hand. The cup of betrothal. By drinking, she indicated that she accepted the will of her father and would marry the carpenter.

She closed her eyes and drank, then returned the cup to her mother's hand and stepped out of the house. She gulped deep breaths of the cool evening air and heard her father's voice: "Has the girl run off again?"

She could not stay here. Her situation had changed too suddenly; her world had become a plank on a storm-tossed sea.

Before her father could call her name, she pulled a clay vessel from the courtyard, opened the gate, and strode toward the village well.

chapter six

The well at Nazareth stood in the northwest corner of town, just outside the city walls. During daylight hours the place served as a social center for townspeople and travelers who passed on the trade route nearby, but the place was deserted when Mary arrived. She set her jug on the ground and let the bucket fall, then slowly pulled it up, allowing some of the cool water to splash her tired feet as she filled her container.

As she set the bucket back on the stone rim, she saw another woman approaching—no, she realized, a girl probably not more than two or three years older. The girl carried a naked baby on one hip and an empty pitcher on the other. From the bulge at the front of her robe, Mary realized the girl was expecting another child.

The girl gave Mary a weary smile, set the crying baby on the wet ground, and proceeded to lower the bucket.

Mary closed her eyes and saw herself coming to this well. By this time next year, she would be living this girl's life; she had no reason or right to expect anything different. She would no longer be under her father's authority but under the carpenter's.

Only time would tell if Joseph would be a loving husband or a domineering one. . . .

She opened her eyes and looked down at the baby—a girl—

to prevent the young mother from seeing her tears. "Hello there," she crooned in falsely bright baby talk. "Would you like to sit on my lap?"

"Leave her," the mother called. "She'll only soil your tunic."

Mary flinched at the sound of the girl's voice. She *knew* this girl, had heard her speak and laugh when the women gathered for the ceremonial *mikvah,* the time of cleansing after their monthly impurity. She had been in the group of girls who married shortly after Naomi, Mary, and Aliyah began to visit the mikvah. . . .

Mary shifted to look into the mother's face. "Judith?"

The girl's sad eyes confirmed their acquaintance. "Mary."

"I haven't seen you in a long time."

A half smile quirked the corner of Judith's mouth. "I've been busy."

"Are you well?"

"Is anyone?"

Mary struggled to find a suitable reply, then reached for the baby. "You don't have to worry about her soiling my tunic—earlier today I managed to do that all by myself."

She bounced the baby on her knee, waiting for Judith to reply, but the young woman poured the last of the water into her jar and hoisted it onto her hip.

"My husband is ill," Judith finally said, regarding Mary with smudges of fatigue beneath her dark eyes. "His parents are dead, and we have no money for the tax tomorrow."

Mary drew a quick breath, then bit her lip. What could she do? She had no money and no hope of getting any. Her betrothed husband might provide a better living than a farmer like her father, but by his choice of mohar he had already proven that he was not a wealthy man. A rich man would have given her a gold bracelet or a circlet of coins intended for her bridal veil, not a simple square of cloth.

"I will ask ADONAI to provide for you," she whispered, returning the baby to her mother.

Judith hesitated, then managed a small smile. "Thank you."

Mary sat in silence and watched them go.

Joseph and his family had left the house by the time Mary returned with the water. Her mother accepted the jug without comment, even though the container against the wall was still more than half full.

"Where is everyone?" Mary asked, helping her mother clear away the remains of the men's dinner. "It is so quiet in here."

"Aaron took the girls to Magdala," her mother replied. "Grandfather Avram is at the synagogue. Your father is there too, probably telling the world about his fine son-in-law."

Her mother left the empty bowls and crossed the room, then pulled the mohar from the shelf where Mary had placed it. She shook out the square of fabric and held it to the light from the window. "It is fine wool." Her voice brimmed with approval. "And the purest white. He must have paid dearly for it."

Mary picked up her father's empty bowl. "It is lovely."

"It will shed rain nicely." Her mother ran her hand over the soft surface. "And the color will keep you cool in the heat."

As Mary stacked the bowls by the basin, she remembered what she'd been about before the world shifted beneath her. "Ruth sent a loaf of her bread," she said, crossing the room to retrieve the package she'd dropped after coming through the door.

Apparently oblivious to Mary's feelings, her mother folded the woolen veil. "Ruth is generous."

Mary's chin trembled. "She is."

"She will miss your help when you have a family of your own."

Mary tried to control herself, but her chin wobbled and her eyes filled in spite of her efforts. Could her mother really be thinking of Ruth at a time like this?

Mary's tears spilled when she looked up and read the answer in her mother's eyes. "Oh, how I will miss you!" She threw her arms around her mother, and for a long moment they stood together, two women bound by blood, experience, and faith.

Mary's mother finally pulled away and cupped her daughter's face between her palms, love burning bright in her magnetic eyes. "I am proud of you, Daughter. Your father may not show it, but he is proud of you too. You will make Joseph ben Jacob a fine wife." Then, with the economy of movement that was part of her nature, she took the bread from Mary and knelt on a straw mat.

Mary sat by her mother's side, knowing her mother would speak freely now that the men had left the house. "Do you think I can be a good wife?"

"Joseph is a good man. It is easy to be a good wife when you are married to a man you respect." Her mother's expression shifted as a wry grin tightened the corner of her mouth. "I was glad your father chose him instead of the silk merchant. Always remember, Daughter, that wealth is not necessary for happiness. It is better to be content and obedient than wealthy."

"This Joseph seems strong . . . like Father. Will he even listen to me?"

A half smile crossed her mother's face. "You will learn how to make him listen. When a man loves a woman as HaShem, blessed be he, loves Isra'el, you will have the power of influence. Use your power wisely, Mary."

Mary set that advice aside for later reference as her mind vibrated with a thousand thoughts. She hugged her bent knees and rested her chin on her arms. "Sometimes life doesn't seem fair. The people of Nazareth have so little, and we women have the hardest lot of all."

"Enough." Her mother looked up, reproach in her eyes. "Would you argue with ADONAI himself?"

"I wouldn't—"

"The man is the lord of the wife, just as ADONAI is lord of the man." She finished unwrapping the bread and gave the crusty surface an appreciative rap with her knuckles. "All we can do is pray for a man who will care for us as ADONAI does."

Mary waited as her mother broke the bread and handed her a piece. "Why . . . why did Father proceed with my betrothal? Why so soon?"

Her mother swallowed hard. "Look around, Daughter. We barely have enough to feed all of us. But Joseph is a strong man, a good man. He will provide for you."

"He's *old*."

Her mother's narrow mouth twisted with humor. "He's not as old as I am, and he is wise. You would not be happy with a foolish boy." She paused. "Something else worries you?"

Mary hesitated. How could she explain the questions whirling in her head and the feelings stirring in her heart? The world outside Nazareth was a cauldron of chaos, and Isra'el's future bleaker than it had been since the Babylonian captivity. Now her people suffered under the domination of Rome and a ruthless Idumaean king, and who could say what horrors the future might bring?

"I will have a family of my own soon," she whispered, "because of Father's choice."

Her mother nodded. "Not only his choice; marriage is the will of ADONAI. And a daughter's duty."

Mary shook her head. "I do not fear marriage, but tonight I watched a girl at the well. She is only a little older than me, but she has nothing to hope for . . . and I fear my children and I will feel the same despair. I want to give my children so much, yet I cannot give them the thing I most long for."

Mary's mother cupped her hand around her daughter's cheek. "And what would you give them?"

"Hope." Mary's voice broke under the weight of the word. "I would give them hope."

Her mother sighed as her thumb caressed Mary's temple. "There is always hope, Mary. We have the word of the prophets and a hope most sure."

"Even in Nazareth?"

"Even here."

chapter seven

The sound of shouting roused Mary from sleep. She pushed herself into a sitting position, then pulled a stray bit of straw from her hair as the noise of creaking bridles and rumbling wheels sifted through the lattice-covered window.

Her mother stood in the doorway, her eyes grim. "Herod's men," she said, crossing her arms. "Come to collect the taxes."

Mary glanced across the room and noticed that Aaron and the girls must have come in after she'd fallen asleep. Her cousins, seven-year-old Hodiya and eight-year-old Hannah, lay sprawled across their straw-stuffed pallets, their arms flung across each other. Aaron, their father, snored against the far wall, covered with a blanket. The family mule stood beside him, contentedly munching the grain in his feed bag.

Mary saw no sign of her father and grandfather. "Have Father and—?"

"Gone to the town center already," her mother finished, keeping her voice low. "So you must stay away from the marketplace today. No respectable woman should go anywhere near the heathen dogs Herod employs."

Mary drew a deep breath as she rose and made her way to the basin. Herod, who called himself king of the Jews, was no son of Isra'el. He had descended from Edomite stock, and though he took great pains not to offend the chief priests and the Temple authorities, no self-respecting Israelite would work for him. Every few months the foreigners he hired as guards and tax collectors moved from village to village, extorting taxes from people who were hard-pressed to feed their children.

Mary poured water onto her hands, then splashed her face with the bracing liquid. Careful not to wake her sleeping cousins, she glanced over her shoulder. "Do you think Joseph will go to the market today?"

Her mother cast a quick, appraising look in Mary's direction before giving her a tight smile. "Joseph is certainly old enough to pay taxes."

"Then . . . perhaps I *should* go out this morning." She caught her mother's warning glance. "Not to walk in view of the guards but to watch my . . . betrothed. Surely I should begin to understand him, since we will be living together."

Her mother considered the idea, her lips pressing into a thin line, and finally she nodded. "You may go," she said, reaching for a veil hanging from a peg on the wall, "but only if I come with you. These are dangerous times, Daughter, and you should not risk your reputation."

"But I am betrothed now—nearly married."

"Which means you must be even more careful to guard your virtue."

Even in a town as small as Nazareth, all communal activity centered on the marketplace. A row of stalls ran the length of the wide main street and offered wares from several merchants. On any other day the men of Nazareth would have allowed their wives and daughters to freely conduct transactions in the marketplace, but this was no ordinary day. With Herod's guards in town, most of the women of Nazareth had been hidden behind veils and courtyard walls. No one wanted to invite unwanted attention.

Mary walked slightly behind her mother with her eyes downcast and her veil tight around her head. Today she would not allow herself to laugh out loud or call to any children she might see in the street. She would become as invisible as possible and speak only when directly addressed.

"I'm beginning to think this was a bad idea," her mother muttered as one of the foreign guards glanced their way. "You could observe Joseph another time. You have months to learn his likes and dislikes; you have a lifetime to know him—"

"Please." Mary caught her mother's arm. "When you were betrothed, did you not yearn to know Father better?"

For an instant her mother's eyes widened; then a reluctant smile crept across her lips. "I suppose I did," she admitted. "The thought of marriage frightened me, but one day I put on my mother's heaviest veil and went to the well, pretending to wait for a friend as I watched your father water the livestock. I sat there over an hour, one eye on him and one on the street that led to our house. I was terrified my father would come searching for me, but he did not."

Comforted by her mother's confession, Mary smiled. "We are much the same, you and I."

"We are both women."

They walked the length of two more houses. Mary's mother put out a hand and stopped. Mary looked up, curious, and her mother gestured toward a house on the opposite side of the merchants' stalls. "Look there."

The small mud dwelling looked much like the others in this part of town, but the owners had hired a worker to install a new door. The carpenter, his bare shoulders shining in the early morning sun, adjusted the leather hinges, then stepped back to test the strength of the latch.

Mary took a wincing little breath when she glimpsed the bearded man's profile. "Joseph."

"Yes." Her mother beamed. "I told you he was a good man. He will be a kind husband to you and a strong father for your children. That one is not afraid of hard labor."

Mary leaned against a courtyard wall and studied her betrothed. Her father might not have consulted her, but he had done well in choosing her husband. Of course, this Joseph might have bad habits she would not discover until later. He might snore, demand that she bring fresh water twice a day, or refuse bread with even a speck of sand in it. But, judging from the lean outline of his frame, he was neither a glutton nor a sluggard. A man did not develop arms like those by sitting and arguing with the rabbis.

And—she felt a warm flush mantle her cheeks—he was a *man*, not a boy. Joseph would not throw seed in her hair or tease her unmercifully or chase her through the fields as Josiah had chased Naomi. Joseph would spend his days thinking about how to ensure his family's survival in a time when desperation could descend as unexpectedly as a summer shower.

"And he is building a house . . . for us," she murmured.

"Yes." Her mother arched a dark brow. "We can walk by it, if you want to. I heard him telling your father where it is—" She turned away as angry voices broke the restive truce between the villagers and the foreigners.

Several paces down the street, one of Herod's men had commandeered a merchant's booth to collect taxes. Several men of Nazareth stood before the booth, including Mary's father.

Anxiety spurted through Mary at the sight of his familiar form.

Her mother tugged at her sleeve. "We must go. Your father will not be pleased to see us here."

"But, Mother! If I am to be a wife, I need to understand these things."

Her mother sighed in exasperation, then yanked on the shoulder of Mary's tunic. "Listen if you must, but not here! Come, we will hide ourselves in the silk merchant's stable."

Mary did not protest as her mother pulled her into the small fenced area behind the merchant's house. Most villagers kept their livestock either in the house or in the courtyard; only families who could afford several animals needed a separate stable.

Mary followed her mother into the pen and knelt beside a startled cow. Through slats in the fence she could view the town center. She strained to listen and pulled her veil across her nose to block the pungent odor of manure.

The villager at the head of the tax line had dropped a coin into the tax collector's hand, but Herod's man had not yet put it away. "My leniency is not appreciated?" he roared. "Did I not ask for two shekels instead of three? Yet you insult my generosity and give me only one."

Frowning, the villager pulled another coin from his purse and set it in the representative's open palm. The tax man—a Celt, by the pale-skinned, blue-eyed look of him—only snorted. When the villager finally gave him a third coin, the Celt tossed the coins onto a pile at his elbow. "Away with you. Next!"

Another villager approached the booth, his head bowed. "I am sorry . . . ," he said, his voice dropping so low Mary could not hear the rest of his statement.

The burly foreigner glared at the man, his teeth gleaming beneath a swath of copper-colored hair. "You Jews always have more than you will admit. Have you a donkey?"

"No, my lord. We have no livestock at all."

"Have you a child?"

The villager took a step back. "Only a daughter. You—you cannot have my child; the Law forbids it."

"I don't want your daughter, but there are Jews in Jerusalem who will pay handsomely for a female slave. Your Law does not forbid you to sell her to your own people, does it?"

Mary pressed her lips together as the poor man shook his head. "She would not work for you; she would only sleep. She is a lazy girl, not fit to work for anyone—"

The tax man gestured to one of Herod's guards. "Go with this man and find his daughter. Pierce her ear with an awl the moment you've secured her; then bring her to me."

The grief-stricken father fell to his knees before the tax collector, but two other guards lifted the man to his feet and shoved him into an alley.

Mary felt her mouth go dry as her father stepped up to the booth. The collector asked his name, and even above the rumble of the cow's belly, Mary heard her father's answer: "Joaquim, son of Judah."

The collector consulted his scroll, then squinted up at Mary's father. "I remember you—we had an agreement from the last collection. If you cannot pay the debt in full today, one-third of the proceeds from your next harvest will be designated for Herod's treasury."

Her father lifted his hands. "If I am so generous to Herod, how am I to feed my family? If I may pay a smaller portion of the tax and work the land for one more season—"

"And how do you intend to pay a portion?"

"My mule." Joaquim clasped his hands. "He is a good animal, and strong."

The tax collector's eyes narrowed. "I see no mule behind you."

"The animal is at home. He is a good pack animal, young, with all his teeth."

The Celt regarded her father with half-closed eyes, then exhaled in a snort. "Bring me the beast straightaway. But next year at this time you will owe double the amount . . . unless you choose to settle your debt now by offering something else?"

Mary closed her eyes as the question hung in the air. Besides the mule, her family owned two goats, a house, and a slender portion of the fields outside Nazareth. Her father also had a wife and a daughter.

Joaquim ben Judah could lose much more than a mule today.

She held her breath until her father replied, "I have nothing else to offer you."

"So we will take the animal. Next time, if you cannot pay a double tax, two-thirds of your crops will be seized for the continued good of King Herod's kingdom."

"Please—" her father's voice dissolved in a thready whisper—"if this season is the same as last—"

"What? You and your family will die?" The tax collector snorted again. "All of us die, Joaquim ben Judah. Some sooner than others."

Her father opened his mouth to answer, but a screaming woman drowned out his reply. The woman ran into the marketplace on the heels of a pair of Herod's guards who were dragging a young woman through the alley.

Mary shrank back against the cow's flank as the woman's shrieking intensified. The weeping girl, who had lost her veil in the struggle, looked out with rounded eyes through a tangle of long hair.

Aliyah.

Mary brought the back of her hand to her mouth as the truth hit her with the force of a blow.

"My daughter!" the woman cried, falling to her knees as she lifted her arms to anyone who would listen. "Please, someone, help us! We have nothing but our daughter, yet Herod would take her from us."

Mary trembled at the unfolding horror. "Mother, can't we—?"

"We should go." Her mother's voice quavered, but she gripped Mary's arm like a vise.

"My child!" the mother screamed again. As Mary watched, the agonized woman rose and charged her husband, falling upon him with surprising vehemence. She beat on her helpless husband's breast while he stood weeping; then both parents sank to the earth and scraped up handfuls of dirt. As they poured sand over their heads and tear-streaked faces, they cried out for mercy, justice, and deliverance.

Mary tore her gaze from the awful picture as her father left the tax collector's booth with empty hands and slumped shoulders. Her uncle Aaron, who must have been expecting this result, led the mule up an alley, handed it to a uniformed guard, and gestured to her father.

Mary's mother set her jaw and pulled her daughter away from the stable-yard fence. "We leave. Now."

"But, Mother, she's my friend—"

"Hush! Someone comes."

They hunched back into their crouched positions as the guard walked the animal toward their hiding place. Another soldier, the man who'd been left to watch over the tethered horses, approached, his hands extended for the mule's reins.

Mary closed her eyes as a pulse of panic played in the pit of her stomach. If they looked toward the stable, she and her mother would be discovered. What would the foreigners do? Laugh, or haul them out before the others?

She opened her eyes in cautious slits as the mule's hooves clip-clopped on the hard ground. The first guard handed the animal over to the other, along with a curt order: "Kill it. We don't need to feed another worthless beast."

Silence as heavy as a wool blanket hung over the house. Mary worked her loom while her mother knelt on the carpet and ground grain. The girls, Hannah and Hodiya, had been told to take the goats to the communal pasture, and Aaron had gone with Grandfather Avram to the synagogue.

Mary's father sat across from her mother, his legs crossed, his empty hands resting on his knees. Ordinarily the house would be crowded with the sounds of the girls' laughter or Mary's singing, but today it was dense with quiet.

Mary checked the threads in her loom and wondered why her father had not joined the other men. He did not usually come home during the day, preferring to spend his time in the fields, at the market, or in the synagogue.

When Mary caught her father looking intently at her mother, she suddenly realized that her presence was an impediment. Her father needed comfort, but he would not admit his need before anyone . . . but his wife.

She set her weaving aside as a blush burned her cheek. How many times had she been oblivious to the unspoken currents that flowed between her parents? There must have been dozens of times they wished to be alone, but Nazareth did not offer many opportunities for privacy.

She slipped from her low stool, plucked her veil from the peg, and murmured something about taking a walk. Her parents did not protest. Herod's hired thugs had left the village, leaving tear-streaked faces and despair in their wake. Several families would be missing members tonight; many children would go to bed hungry. Wives would try to console their husbands, who would rant or curse by turn, helpless to spare their families grief or control their destinies.

Outside her gate, Mary turned to the right and walked at a brisk pace, careful to remain inside the ribbon of shade cast by the setting sun. Several women worked in their courtyards, milking their goats or gathering wood for their cook fires. She nodded soberly at one of her mother's friends and was about to ask how the family had fared with the taxes, but the sound of an approaching man and beast made her lower her head.

She turned away as prickles of uneasiness nipped at the back of her neck. What if this was a straggler from Herod's company? What if the man was drunk? She should not be out here alone.

"Mary?"

Surprised that a man would speak to her, she turned . . . and saw the stranger who was now her husband. Joseph stood in the street, holding the reins of a mule. Her *father's* mule.

Her eyes widened. "How—?"

Joseph offered her the reins. "A soldier's thirst for bloodshed is outweighed only by his hunger for silver."

Momentarily speechless, Mary took the reins and looked into Joseph's arresting face. The words *thank you* were appropriate for this moment, but they felt insufficient to convey the gratitude stirring her soul.

What was wrong with her? She ought to feel comfortable with this man. She ought to speak freely with him, but for some reason she could not bring herself to voice the emotions at the core of her being.

If Joseph saw the tumult in her eyes, kindness compelled him to ignore it. "And how is your father?"

"He is well." She swallowed hard and found it easy to talk about trivial matters. "He and my mother were deep in conversation when I left. I am sure they will search for some way to pay the taxes."

Joseph slipped his hands through the rope belt tied at his waist. "Tell your father Herod's men left the animal behind. Which, I suppose, they did. And ask if he and your uncle are available to help me tomorrow. The town elders have asked me to build a new gate for the wall."

When she hesitated, blinking with bafflement, his wide mouth curved in a one-sided smile. "A man needs his pride, Mary."

"Thank you." The words spilled from her lips. "Thank you, thank you, thank you . . . Joseph."

This time the smile he gave her reached his eyes and warmed her heart.

chapter eight

The next morning, Mary gave Hannah and Hodiya an extra helping of bread and butter, then pulled her shawl tighter around her shoulders and thrust another branch onto the smoldering embers in the center of the house.

Her parents, uncle, and grandfather had been huddled around a fire in the courtyard since just after sunrise, trying to devise some means to increase the family's income. Mary, who would be counted among Joseph's family at the next tax-collection day, had been excused from the discussion, though her father had told her to thank Joseph for his offer. He and Aaron would be pleased to help build the new city gates.

Though the thought of separating from her family still brought pain, Mary couldn't deny that marriage might bring unique opportunities. Life in Nazareth was not easy for anyone, but didn't the Torah teach that trials served to strengthen one's endurance? Job endured testing in order to exercise his faith and deepen his humility. David committed serious sins and suffered many hardships, yet the Scriptures described him as a man "after God's own heart."

If her marriage to Joseph brought hard times and struggles . . . might not those difficulties strengthen her faith? Mary looked through the window and saw her parents' earnest faces. They worked hard; they shivered in the morning cold and often went to sleep without having their hunger satisfied, yet they faithfully went to the synagogue and prayed for the deliverance of Isra'el. They believed deliverance would come, too, just as the prophets had predicted.

Her parents were not the only people who had suffered. She had been only four years old when Aaron brought his bride home. Tirza had warmed the house with her laughter, and they had all rejoiced when Hannah and Hodiya were born.

With the birth of each daughter, Mary had climbed into her uncle's arms and asked if he was disappointed the baby wasn't a boy. "Disappointed? Of course not!" he'd replied. "I want a house filled with baby girls as pretty as my beautiful niece."

The following year, in the darkness of an icy night, Tirza gave birth to a boy who died before his naming and circumcision. Mary had stood in the shadows, her heart aching as her lively, adoring uncle hid his face in his hands and wept.

The year after Aaron's son died, Tirza birthed a girl who lived only thirty days. During that winter many babies died from a cough that swept through Nazareth and claimed the lives of young and old alike.

In Mary's eighth summer, Tirza died while trying to give birth to a baby that remained hidden until the midwife cut the child from its lifeless mother. Mary had sheltered Hannah and Hodiya from the bloody sight as Aaron tore his robes and Grandfather Avram wailed in grief.

A breeze blew by the window, and something in the sound tore at Mary's heart. When she was married and living in Joseph's house, would she face despair like her parents and uncle had known? Would she hold lifeless babies in her arms? If her infants survived, would they grow into children who looked at her with hunger in their eyes? Would Joseph have to hide their sons and daughters so they would not be sold into slavery?

She could not stop thinking about Aliyah. In an instant, everything had changed for the shy girl who had dreamed of marrying the rabbi's son. She had awakened yesterday a much-loved daughter; she had gone to sleep—if she *could* sleep—as a slave.

Mary shuddered. She would rather be barren like her kinswoman Elizabeth than watch her children be taken to serve a heathen king. She would rather throw herself on a sword than see them pierced and prodded by Herod's foreign henchmen.

She pulled her knees to her chest and poked at the fire with a stick. A plume of gray smoke rose in the center of the house, accompanied by a whispering and crackling, as though the fire mocked her thoughts. . . .

Mary stood, suddenly uncomfortable in the smoky space.

"Hannah—" she pressed her hand to the top of her cousin's dark head—"will you and Hodiya promise to be quiet while I take a walk?"

The girl lifted her chin and smiled, her new teeth too big for her small face. "Will you be gone long?"

"I thought I might walk in the olive grove. Perhaps, if you are good, I can bring you some olives."

Hodiya dipped her index finger in the crock of goat's butter, then licked it. "We will be good."

"I know you will. Your father is outside if you need him."

Mary pulled her veil over her head and stepped through the doorway. Her mother turned, a question in her eyes, but Mary gestured to the street and waved, silently promising to return soon.

Out on the slanting street, she inhaled a deep breath of fresh air and lengthened her stride. The sunrise had painted a rosy flush on the western mountains, and a sweet breeze ruffled the treetops. Life stirred in every house, but few people would be heading for the fields or the marketplace before they'd broken their fast.

She pulled her veil around her neck to ward off the morning chill and headed toward the city gates. She would visit her favorite place, the spot she'd come to regard as her own special retreat. In truth, the ancient grove belonged to the entire village, but not many people visited it except during harvesttime.

She crested a hill from which she could see the countryside beyond the city walls. Already the fields basked in sunshine that hinted of a scorching day to come. The view vanished as Mary traversed another street, silently hurrying past mud houses crowded together at odd angles, properties defined by cactus hedges, courtyards, and vine-covered walls.

The city watchmen were opening the rickety gates as she drew near. One of the elders raised a bushy brow at her approach, but she gave him a quick smile and waited until the gates had been secured before she slipped out of the village and walked into the grove.

The deep shade beneath the old trees calmed her at once. Several of the harvesters' nets still hung from the lower branches, a few overripe olives dotting the fine mesh. She moved among the trees, ducking under the nets, as the trees lifted gnarled fingers and pointed to the heavens.

In some ways, though it would pain her father to know it, she thought this a more holy place than the Temple in Jerusalem. Herod had rebuilt the Temple, and though it had been designed to be magnificent and awe inspiring, she felt closer to ADONAI in this garden of hundred-year-old trees. In this quiet place she did not have to contend with money changers or chanting priests, nor did she have to restrict herself to a place designated for women. Here she could wander as she pleased, lifting her eyes to the leafy canopy as she reflected on the words of David, Isra'el's greatest king:

> *I am like an olive tree,*
> *thriving in the house of God.*
> *I trust in God's unfailing love*
> *forever and ever.*
> *I will praise you forever, O God,*
> *for what you have done.*
> *I will wait for your mercies*
> *in the presence of your people.*

Mary ran her hands over her arms, hugging herself as the music of the woods joined in her anthem of praise. A gentle wind blew through the branches overhead like a silken whisper, and she smiled when the whisper became a word . . . and a greeting.

"Hail, O favored one."

Mary's delight shifted to uneasiness. This was no trick of the wind; this was *language*.

"The Lord is with you."

She halted, her sense of uneasiness turning into a deeper and more immediate fear. Had she trespassed upon some holy place? Had she offended ADONAI with her thoughts about the Temple?

Slowly she turned, about to flee the garden, but a stranger stood in her path. Taller than her father, his eyes burned at the level of many of the tallest branches, and his skin glowed with a radiance brighter than the hottest fire. He was neither Hebrew nor Celt nor Roman. He was unlike any man she had ever seen. Could he be . . . something other than a man?

No. Daniel had seen an angel, and Abraham and Jacob, but they were holy men and leaders of Isra'el. Who was she but a poor and simple girl?

When a frightened squeak escaped her lips, her visitor smiled. "Greetings, favored woman. The Lord is with you."

Gripped by a tremor of mingled fear and anticipation, Mary stared at the stranger.

"Don't be frightened, Mary," the man went on, his voice brimming with power, "for I am Gabriel, and I stand in the very presence of God. It was he who sent me to bring you this good news."

A bead of perspiration traced a cold trail from her armpit to her rib. What news could he be talking about?

He leaned forward, an intense light pouring through his eyes. "God has decided to bless you. You will become pregnant and have a son, and you are to name him Jesus. He will be very great and will be called the Son of the Most High. The Lord God will give him the throne of his ancestor David. He will reign over Isra'el forever; his kingdom will never end."

Somehow Mary remained on her feet, though a subterranean quiver rose from her center and threatened to unhinge her bones. "But . . . how can I have a baby? I am a virgin. I have known no man."

A glimmer of unguarded awe shone in the angel's eyes. "The Holy Spirit will come upon you, and the power of the Most High will overshadow you. So the baby born to you will be holy, and he will be called the Son of God."

Mary took a deep breath and felt a dozen different emotions collide. "The Son . . . of God?"

Gabriel must have intuited her confusion, for his lips curved in an understanding smile. "What's more, your relative Elizabeth has become pregnant in her old age. People used to call her barren, but she's already in her sixth month. For nothing, Mary, is impossible with God."

Mary stared at the angelic visitor, her heart pounding. After a long moment, she slipped to her knees. Like David and Abraham and Jacob, she would trust the word of ADONAI. "I am the Lord's servant," she whispered, "and I am willing to accept whatever he wants. May everything you have said come true."

The angel dipped his head as an owl swooped toward her from one of the trees. Mary's eyes followed the bird for only an instant, but when she looked for the angel, he had . . . vanished.

She remained on her knees in a quiet that felt thicker than it had before; then she lowered herself to the moss-carpeted earth and spread her hands as she whispered the prayer of her heart.

"I am ADONAI's servant," she repeated, "and I am willing."

chapter nine

In the dazzling white sunlight of Jerusalem, Herod the Great squinted with approval at the stonemasons maneuvering marble blocks into position. His chief architect stood nearby, an unfurled diagram in hand, while Tero, the king's counselor, frowned at the retinue loitering in the shade.

"The aqueduct," the architect said, a quaver in his voice, "will be as tall as ten men. More magnificent than even those of Rome." The thin man tried to smile, but the corners of his mouth only wobbled as he offered the diagram to his king.

Herod leaned forward and glanced at the sketch. "Make it as tall as fifteen men. The new fountains will need water, as will those of the palace garden." He glanced at his advisor. "What say you, Tero? The aqueducts at Caesarea would make a fine model, no?"

Tero bowed his head, a smile finding its way through his mask of annoyance. "Caesarea is a model city, Excellency. Caesar should be proud to have it bear his name."

"I imagine he is. If only he would come to see it for himself." Herod turned his attention back to the architect's drawing. "Now, about these sculptures . . ."

The man barreled his narrow chest. "They will be the largest in Jerusalem."

"I want them covered with gold." When Herod lifted his head, he caught the worried glance the architect threw at Tero. The man would be concerned about cost, certainly, but puny minds always worried about puny matters.

Tero smoothed the pleats of the toga draped over his arm. "Your Excellency knows that to acquire this much gold will not be an easy feat."

"And that is why I have loyal subjects," Herod answered, gesturing to the walkway that led back into the shade of the palace. "Come, let us get out of this sun."

He led the way, allowing his counselor to walk by his side as the rest of his attendants followed. "The tax collection in the northern kingdom," he said, pitching his voice for Tero's ear alone. "Any sign of rebellion?"

Tero smiled without humor. "None that remain."

Herod lifted a brow. "So there were rebels?"

"No one that need worry the king. No organized movements, only a few religious zealots. No one strong enough to provide any resistance."

Herod halted and faced his counselor. "And what of the people and their prophecy? their awaited Messiah?" He glanced behind him as the retinue halted beyond the range of hearing. "Was the prophecy the cause of their dissention?"

A flicker of unease moved in the depths of his advisor's eyes. "The prophecy is only a myth, Your Excellency. Trite words handed down by those unwise enough to accept their true king."

Herod considered Tero's reply, then gestured to the walkway again. "Send my guard back to the nests of rebellion," he said, lengthening his stride. "Find the families that spawned the rebels and strike at them until not even a cousin's cousin remains. We must pluck out opposition by the root."

Before his counselor could spin away, Herod caught the sleeve of Tero's tunic and halted in midstep. "A king does not reign for more than thirty years by ignoring threats. What would be unwise, my loyal counselor, is to take such a prophecy too lightly."

Tero drew a tight smile over his protruding front teeth and bowed low. "As always, my king, you are a fount of wisdom."

chapter **ten**

Though the calm and cool evening was as sweet as an evening could be, Mary passed a restless night. She was not surprised when she heard rustling from the men's side of the room until well after dark. At dinner, anxiety over the taxes had shadowed both her father and Uncle Aaron. But when the men finally eased into sleep, she remained awake, one hand pressed to the lightly concave area that lay between her jutting hip bones.

How would the promised miracle happen? Did Gabriel mean she would bear a child within the next year or within twenty? Would she puff up as suddenly as one of the camel bladders the children inflated to play kickball, or would she bear this promised child in the normal way of women?

She turned onto her side and pillowed her cheek on her hand. A few feet away, a sliver of moonlight lit her mother's dreaming face. She would give anything to be able to reach out, wake her mother, and share what had happened in the olive grove. But though her mother devoutly followed ADONAI, she was also extremely pragmatic. She would find it difficult to accept that the messenger of God had come to visit her daughter. She'd find it even harder to believe that Mary would one day have a child begotten not of man but of the *Ruach HaKodesh*, or Spirit of God. She'd find it *impossible* to believe that Mary's miracle child would grow up to be the Messiah, the hope of Isra'el.

How could the King of the Universe spring from a family too poor to pay its taxes? How could she explain these things to her parents? How could she understand them herself?

Perhaps she wasn't meant to understand. The thoughts of the Almighty were high above man's thoughts, his ways far beyond human understanding.

"'There are three things that amaze me,'" she whispered, recalling the words of a proverb, "'no, four things I do not understand: how an eagle glides through the sky, how a snake slithers on a rock, how a ship navigates the ocean, how a man loves a woman.'"

Now there are five: how the Master of the Universe, blessed be he, could take notice of me.

Mary rolled onto her stomach, then rested her cheek on her arms. How would this news affect her marriage? Would Joseph need to be told? Or would ADONAI arrange something to take Joseph out of her life? If HaShem, blessed be his name, didn't need a man to conceive this special child, perhaps Mary wasn't meant to be married. Perhaps she wasn't supposed to have a family . . . or any other children.

She sighed as an odd twinge of disappointment struck. The angel's incredible news was a privilege too great to comprehend, but as honored as she would be to bear this Holy One, she had always wanted a houseful of children. She loved the noise and commotion of Ruth's house, and even the Scriptures said that children were a blessing from ADONAI. Happy was the man who had a quiver full of them. . . .

Her conscience rose in the darkness and shook a wagging finger. Now she was being foolish . . . and perhaps even ungrateful. HaShem, blessed be his name, had chosen her for this task, so he would enable her to complete it.

She closed her eyes and prayed that ADONAI would reveal exactly how she was supposed to do so much with so little.

The next morning, after sweeping the house and preparing breakfast for Hannah and Hodiya, Mary returned to the olive grove in the hope that she'd hear from the angel again. She waited over an hour, but only the wind and the trees kept her company.

While she sat in the stillness, however, a memory she had shoved aside resurfaced: *"Your relative Elizabeth has become pregnant in her old age."*

The messenger of God had given her a way to prove his words, so she would visit her cousin before telling anyone about the angel's prophecy. When she could report that aged, barren Elizabeth had given birth to a child, Mary's family would know that ADONAI was working in their midst.

She hurried home and moved through the routine of her day, searching for the right moment to approach her family. She milked the goats, skimmed the milk, and delivered two cheeses to the rabbi's family. She lingered by the town center and chatted with several of the women. She carried water from the well, delivered lunch to her father at the gate and her uncle and grandfather in the fields, then returned home to work her loom under her mother's watchful gaze.

As the day drew to a close, she set a platter of bread, olives, and cheese before her father, uncle, and grandfather. They sat, heavy lidded and tired from a full day's work, on straw mats in the lattice-patterned light.

Mary stood back, waiting for the men to begin eating, and glanced across the room. Her mother stood at the window, a bowl of parched grain in her hands. The girls, who'd eaten earlier, played with straw dolls out in the courtyard.

"The night comes quickly," her mother said, turning her attention back to the men, "with the scent of rain in the wind."

"Good." Mary's grandfather broke the bread, then lifted his hands to offer the traditional prayer of thanksgiving: *"Baruch Atah ADONAI Elohenu Melech Ha'olam, hamotzi Lechem Min Ha'aretz."* Blessed are you, Lord our God, King of the Universe, who brings forth bread from the earth.

Mary waited until her father had taken his first bite before kneeling at his side. "Forgive me for interrupting," she said, looking at her hands, "but I would like to visit my cousin Elizabeth. I was hoping to leave tomorrow."

Her father stopped chewing.

Mother was so startled she forgot her place. "Elizabeth?" She stepped forward and stared at her daughter. "Whatever for?"

Mary studied her work-worn hands. They were ordinary hands, just as she was an ordinary girl. But ADONAI had asked her to live something other than an ordinary life . . . and she had promised to be willing.

"I must soon go live with Joseph," Mary said, choosing her words with care. "Before I become attached to a husband, I'd like to go stay with Elizabeth for a few weeks."

Her father drew a deep breath, but her mother was quicker to voice her thoughts. "Have you had words with Joseph? Has he put some kind of pressure on you?"

Mary shook her head.

"If he is pressuring you," her father said, his voice grave, "you could go live with him at any time. There is no shame in a man's desire for his wife."

Mary felt her cheeks burn. "I have not talked to Joseph since he returned the mule," she said, daring to meet her mother's penetrating gaze. "I am speaking of my own wish. I would like to visit Elizabeth before Joseph comes . . . before we are married."

Her parents looked at each other while her uncle ate in silence, curiosity and mischief gleaming from his eyes. Later, Mary suspected, he would tease her, desperate to know the reason for her sudden yearning to leave home.

Not even her doting uncle would believe the true story.

"This is a foolish idea," her father said. "Elizabeth has no need for you to visit. She is an old woman."

"She has said I am welcome at any time," Mary pointed out. "The last time we visited, she said I could return."

"It is time for the barley harvest," Mother said. "We need your help in the fields."

"The barley, what little there was, has been brought in." Mary lifted her chin. "And four months remain before the wheat harvest."

"Elizabeth would not wish for you to travel alone, and we cannot take you." Her father folded his arms, confident in his argument. "She would think you crazy for even suggesting the idea."

She will not think I am crazy. Mary looked from parent to parent, wondering how far she dared push them. "I've already made inquiries, and I believe I've found a way I can go. Sarah and Jacob are leaving for Jerusalem in the morning. I've told Sarah I could help with her children on the journey . . . with your blessing, of course."

This time when her parents looked at each other, a silent understanding seemed to pass between them. "She will soon be married," her mother murmured, shrugging. "A busy wife has no time to visit relatives."

The straight line of her father's shoulders drooped slightly. He reached for an olive. "How long would you be gone?"

Mary pressed her lips together. "As long . . . as long as I am welcome. As long as Elizabeth needs me."

A worry line appeared on her uncle's forehead. "The last time you visited, you stayed an entire summer."

"I will come back soon enough, Uncle. After all, I have promised to help with the harvest. And I have made another promise . . . to Joseph ben Jacob."

Her father sucked at the inside of his cheek for a moment, his thick brows working. He knew she was not eager to be married. . . . Did he think she was looking for a way of escape?

"Make certain," Uncle Aaron said, his voice gruff, "that Zechariah finds a good family for you to travel with on the journey home."

A heavy silence filled the room; then Grandfather Avram cleared his throat. "And what do we say to the young man when he asks after you? Does Joseph know you plan to go away?"

"Not yet."

"Will you tell him?"

Mary closed her eyes, bracing herself for the inevitable. "I will."

Early the next morning, Mary found her betrothed working at the silk merchant's stable. The aged fence she had hidden behind was being replaced by a structure of wood and stone that looked far sturdier.

As her promised husband crouched beside the fence, she stood in the street and thrust her hands into her sleeves. The bright sunlight threw broken shadows onto Joseph's back and shoulders, but the rails shaded his face.

She hesitated, not sure how to proceed. "Joseph?"

He lifted his head and stood, greeting her with a slow smile. "Mary! I did not expect to see you here."

"I did not expect to come. But something has come up and I . . ." She faltered, not knowing how to give him unwelcome news.

His eyes were dark in the bright sunlight, unreadable. "You have something to tell me?"

"I am going away."

Was that a flicker of disappointment on his face . . . or irritation?

He wiped his brow with a cloth, then gestured to a spot of shade under a thatched roof. "Would you like to sit?"

"I'm sorry, but Jacob and Sarah are preparing to leave for Jerusalem and I've promised to go with them. Before I left, though, I wanted to tell you—"

"You're leaving?" His voice was clipped.

"I will be back."

When he looked at her with that dark and inscrutable gaze, she felt like an inexperienced child. What was this man thinking? He was not like her uncle, whose moods she could read like the sky, or her father, who spoke his mind without hesitation. She could see thought working behind Joseph's deep eyes, yet she had no idea what he would say next.

He looked away and cleared his throat. "If you are unhappy about our betrothal—"

She lifted her hand, eager to correct his misconception. "I'm not unhappy. My father has decided for me, and I trust him. I know you are a good man. When the time comes, I will go willingly with you to your father's house. Unless . . . *you* have objections."

She thought of the few belongings she had placed in her traveling bag and how she had chosen to leave the square of white wool, Joseph's gift, at home . . . in case he changed his mind.

His eyes narrowed slightly as he searched her face, and she

winced when suspicion entered his expression. Did he think she loved someone else?

"I am not running from anything," she hurried to explain. "I am going to Juttah, near Maon, to visit my cousin Elizabeth. I have heard that she . . . well, she may need me."

"Juttah?" Joseph frowned. "That is a five- or six-day journey."

"I am strong." Mary lowered her gaze from his burning eyes. "And I will return by the time of the wheat harvest." She forced a smile and gestured toward the unfinished fence. "I may be back before you have finished here."

Joseph snorted with the half-choked mirth of a man who rarely laughed, then wiped his hands on a cloth at his belt. "If you *should* go, you *must* go. I will finish this fence and continue my work on our house. You may be surprised, Mary, at how much a man can accomplish when his heart is in his work."

Aware of the slender, delicate thread that bound them, Mary smiled and took a step back. "May ADONAI watch between us while we are apart."

"May he bless and watch over *you*, Mary."

She gave him one last smile, then turned toward the well, where Jacob and Sarah waited.

The great caravan route that began at Acco on the sea divided into two branches a few miles beyond its origination. The northern road continued straightaway to Caesarea Philippi, but the southern road, which the Romans called *Via Maris*, dipped and rambled through Galilee, passing by Nazareth on its way south. The ancient route then traversed Nain before wending northward toward Cana, Magdala, and Gennesaret. At the north end of the Sea of Galilee, the road rejoined its more direct offshoot and continued to Damascus.

The many sights and sounds of the Via Maris never failed to amaze Mary. They shared the highway with camel caravans laden with treasures from the East, military mule trains, and scores of ordinary people traveling with donkeys. Hebrews, Greeks, Romans, and sloe-eyed men from the East passed their party, filling her ears with foreign tongues and her eyes with unfamiliar sights.

Mary and her fellow travelers made good time until the Via Maris veered toward the north, just past Nain. At that point, they turned onto the highway that led to Jerusalem—a road even more heavily traveled and far more dusty.

They would not, Jacob reported, be traveling through Samaria. An open hostility existed between the Samaritans and the children of Isra'el, so they would travel east, go south through Peraea, and cross the Jordan before reaching Jericho. Jerusalem lay only a few miles beyond Jericho, and Juttah only a few miles past the Holy City.

Mary accepted Jacob's plan and tried not to think of the miles stretching ahead of them. They would be covering most of the distance in the early morning and late-afternoon hours, in order to avoid the heat of the day. They would sleep either by the side of the road or, if they were near a hospitable village, in the homes of strangers who remembered the Torah's admonition to "be not forgetful to entertain strangers."

As the man charged with the protection of the women and children, Jacob grew noticeably nervous as they walked over the southern highway. The Roman soldiers garrisoned at Jerusalem and Caesarea frequently patrolled these roads, riding by in gleaming chariots that forced pedestrians off the pavement. Tax collectors set up tables whenever and wherever they liked, imposing bridge tolls, road taxes, and town dues. Many of the taxes were supposed to be levied only on merchants who carried their wares from city to city, but because the tax men claimed they could not tell a traveler from a merchant, they frequently taxed every item in a traveler's possession.

Mary had been dreading the sight of soldiers and tax collectors, but they had traveled only a short distance before they met a group of pilgrims resting at a well. The travelers, from the Galilean village of Cana, were more than happy to have the group from Nazareth join them on the road to Jerusalem. The larger the group, Mary realized, the less likely they were to be harassed on the journey.

Before setting out, though, the social niceties had to be observed. Each party had to ask the other where they were from, where they were going, who were their parents, how many children did they have, what were their names, and from what tribe did they descend. By the time they were finally ready to move on, the sun had slanted from the eastern sky to the western.

After helping Sarah's children into the wooden box that fit atop their donkey's blanket, Mary turned and saw an older woman struggling to lift a waterskin onto her shoulder. "Let me help you." Mary dropped her own bundle to assist the woman.

The woman grunted her thanks, then studied Mary with narrowed eyes. "From Nazareth, are you?"

"Yes."

"Going to Jerusalem?"

"To Juttah, to visit a kinswoman."

The woman nodded and gestured to a small donkey tied to a tree. "Put your pack on his back if you like, and walk with my daughters. You'll be well watched over."

"Thank you." Mary bowed in respect, then went to join the others. As much as she enjoyed Sarah's children, lately something in her had been yearning for the company and conversation of women.

chapter eleven

After six days on the road, Mary's feet were blistered and her bones ached, but at last the band of travelers neared Jerusalem. Since Jacob and Sarah planned to proceed to the Holy City, Jacob found Mary a place with a group journeying to Juttah, a small village in the hill country. The remaining distance, Jacob assured her, was not great. She would arrive at her cousin's village by midday.

After entering the gates of Juttah, Mary said her farewells to her escorts and lingered at the well, pulling up the bucket for a drink and an opportunity to splash her hands, face, and feet. The women of the village had retreated behind their lattice-covered windows, for no one willingly carried water in the heat of the afternoon.

As she dried her wet hands on her tunic, Mary glanced around the village. She'd been with her family the last time she visited her cousin's house. She'd been younger in those days and so caught up in her relatives' stories and laughter that she paid little attention to her surroundings.

Now she had no idea how to find Elizabeth's house. She could start walking and hope to find it in a random search, or she could sit at the well and wait for the women to venture from their houses. But the sun had barely passed its zenith, so she might be waiting a long time.

Her queasy stomach settled the question for her. Overcome by a sudden wave of nausea, she crouched by the side of the well and braced her shoulder against the stones, staring out at streets that shimmered in the heat haze. Her skin pearled with perspiration, and her mind drifted into a fuzzy fog as the questions she'd pondered for the last week whirled in her head.

From out of nowhere, a little girl ambled by, then stopped to stare at the stranger by the well.

Mary blinked to be sure her eyes weren't playing tricks on her. When the child didn't vanish like a mirage, she summoned what she hoped was a disarming smile. "Hello. Can you tell me how to get to the house of Zechariah the priest?"

The little girl eyed her with a suspicious squint. "I don't know him."

"Perhaps you know his wife, Elizabeth. She must come here to draw water."

The girl's forehead puckered. "The old woman?"

"Yes, she's older."

"The one with no children?"

Mary grimaced as a small dart of despair pierced her heart. How Elizabeth must have suffered if even the children of this village knew of her fruitless womb! But, ADONAI be praised, Elizabeth was barren no longer.

"Yes," she said, firming her voice. "She's the woman I want to see."

The girl pointed to a side street. "Down there."

"Thank you."

Despite her weariness, Mary's pulse quickened as she neared the foliage-covered walls. How would she explain this unannounced visit? Should she act surprised to see that her kinswoman was expecting a child?

How much did Elizabeth know . . . and how much could she accept?

Mary paused before the gated courtyard, where a broad-leaved vine crawled up the wall and spilled blue flowers over the entry. She remembered this house and especially the kind countenance of the woman who lived within. Elizabeth was a woman of faith. No matter what Mary told her, she would believe.

Mary summoned her courage and called out a greeting. "Elizabeth?"

Deep inside the house, safely tucked into the shade, Elizabeth braced herself against the wall and stared at the bulge of her belly. There! A definite kick and twist! The babe had quickened several weeks earlier, but today he seemed to be turning head over heels.

"Elizabeth?" the voice called again, summoning another joyous kick from the baby within her.

Elizabeth released a throaty laugh and pushed herself up from her bench, then smiled as the Ruach HaKodesh revealed the reason for her unborn son's acrobatics.

The mother of her Lord had come.

Mary blinked in the dim light, then knelt at Elizabeth's side. "It is true," she whispered, peering at the pronounced mound beneath the older woman's tunic. "You *are* with child."

Elizabeth gasped, her eyes widening.

Mary reached for her cousin's arm. "Are you all right? Should I get help?"

"I am fine—more than fine. I am blessed. My son is active today." Elizabeth reached out and tenderly traced Mary's cheek. "Blessed are you among women, dear one . . . and blessed is the fruit of your womb."

Mary sat back, stunned beyond words. "How—?"

"What an honor this is, that the mother of my Lord should visit me." Elizabeth's bright eyes filled with tears as she sank to a low stool. "When you came in and greeted me, my baby jumped for joy. You are blessed, because you believed that the Lord would do what he said."

Mary gazed at Elizabeth for a long moment, her own heart filling with wonder. She'd come a long way, expecting ADONAI to reveal a pregnant kinswoman, and he had done so much more! He had validated his word about Elizabeth; he had proven his promise that she would bear the Messiah—and he had done these things without requiring her to utter a word of explanation.

"Oh, how I praise the Lord," Mary said, lifting her arms as she raised her gaze to the heavens. "How I rejoice in God my Savior! For he took notice of his lowly servant girl, and now generation after generation will call me blessed. For he, the Mighty One, is holy, and he has done great things for me."

Elizabeth nodded, her arms caressing her unborn son, as Mary's song of praise filled the humble house.

That night, after the evening meal, Elizabeth sat with Mary by the window while Zechariah knelt in prayer.

"My husband is quite attentive," Elizabeth said, a small smile playing at the corner of her mouth. "He wanted to hire a servant to help me during the day, but I told him ADONAI would provide a companion for me." She squeezed Mary's shoulder. "And here you are."

Mary studied the priest, whose lips moved soundlessly as he prayed. "Does he not speak at all?"

"He has been silent since he came out of the Holy Place. Since he doubted the will of God."

Mary lifted a brow. "How do you know—?"

"He has written everything that happened that day. An angel appeared to him in the Holy Place and told him I would bear a son . . . and that we should name him John. Our son will be great in the eyes of the Lord, and he will turn many Israelites to ADONAI." Her eyes grew thoughtful. "He will prepare the way for *your* son."

Mary could not speak; her heart was too full.

Elizabeth smiled at her husband. "Zechariah told the angel we were too old for children . . . and he has been silent ever since."

Mary reached for Elizabeth's hand. "HaShem, blessed be he, will lift his burden."

"God will always do what is right. But Zechariah feels unworthy of having his burden lifted. He feels he has disappointed the Lord."

Mary watched the priest offer his evening prayers. Hard to believe that one so holy could disappoint ADONAI, but if Zechariah could fail, so could she.

Elizabeth lifted Mary's hand, then turned it so that it lay flat against her palm. "So young," she said simply, comparing her age-speckled hand to her kinswoman's younger one. She met Mary's eyes. "Are you frightened?"

Mary hesitated, then nodded.

"God has graced you with a child," Elizabeth said, her voice firm. "He will protect both of you, just as he has protected me. Last night I prayed that ADONAI would give this body of mine just a little more strength for these long days—"

"I cannot tell anyone." Words bubbled to Mary's lips. "You know Mother. Father. They will not believe my story."

"But they love you."

"Yes . . . but—"

"You have great faith, Mary. Trust ADONAI. He is not asking you to convince them."

Mary lowered her gaze. Elizabeth found it easy to believe, for the Lord had quickened her womb in another miracle, but her mother had experienced no miracles, nothing but hardship and suffering.

Elizabeth tapped her hand. "The ones I've told of what happened in the Temple? Some believe; some don't. The choice is theirs to make."

Mary nodded slowly. "There is something else I don't understand."

Elizabeth bent her head toward Mary, her eyes alight with question.

"I will gladly carry out whatever ADONAI asks of me," Mary continued, "but why did he ask *me* to do this? I am nothing."

Elizabeth laughed softly, pressing Mary's hand between both of her own. "You are everything, dear one. You are the daughter of Eve whose offspring will crush the serpent's head. The fact that you do not believe yourself worthy of this honor assures me that HaShem, blessed be he, has chosen wisely."

"The angel said my son would be King over the house of Jacob."

Elizabeth drew a deep breath. "What I felt . . . the joy my baby felt . . . was not for an earthly king." She released Mary's hand. "Your son will reign over the house of Jacob and the throne of David, but he is the one Isaiah called the 'righteous branch.' The name given to him will be *ADONAI Tzidkenu*, the Lord is our Righteousness."

Mary sat in silence, absorbing this news. The *how* and *who* and *why* still perplexed her, but she was content to remain a simple woman and let ADONAI maintain his mysteries.

Yet she would have to face other concerns, earthly matters, in the weeks ahead.

"There is something else." She searched Elizabeth's lined face, wishing she could tap into the older woman's wisdom. "My father has chosen a husband for me. He is preparing our home."

"Your baby will need a father."

"But—" Mary swallowed hard and bit back tears—"the Law says I am to remain pure until I am wed. How is Joseph to believe . . . this?"

Elizabeth smiled as the implications of that statement resonated in their shared space. When anxious tears filled Mary's eyes, Elizabeth pulled her head to her shoulder. "Ah, do not worry, little one. Stay as long as you wish. Rejoice with us. ADONAI will answer these questions for you . . . in his time."

Mary sniffed and swiped at her cheeks, reveling in the comfort of the older woman's embrace.

"How kind ADONAI is, to choose us to do his will," Elizabeth continued, her voice as warm as the heat radiating from the embers of her cook fire. "He has taken away my disgrace of having no children. And from now on, all people will call you blessed."

Mary listened but couldn't help wondering what would happen when she returned to Nazareth. Zechariah, one of the most devout and blameless priests she knew, had failed God. Despite this great honor, in spite of all God had promised to do, could she yet fail the Almighty in her task? And what of Joseph? That good man could not be avoided forever.

These questions lingered at the edge of her mind like the darkness looming outside the warm, cozy house.

chapter twelve

A thin ribbon of sweat wandered down Anna's back as she searched for the spot. On a hilly street, Joaquim had said. Next to Jacob's house.

The sound of pounding hammers led her to the place. Joseph had chosen to build his new house next to his father's, but she would have known the structure belonged to a carpenter no matter where she had found it. Wide wooden beams framed the sills of two windows—two!—and a strong lintel marked the place where a solid door would rest. Joseph had already begun to gather stones to build a courtyard wall, and Anna could close her eyes and envision Mary standing in front of this house, feeding her goats and watching her children. . . .

She opened her eyes as the sound of hammering stopped. Joseph stood in the doorway, wiping sweat from his brow as he peered at her.

She took a step forward and lifted the wrapped package in her hand. "Greetings, Joseph. I have brought you a cheese."

He came forward with an eager step. "Thank you. Have you word from Mary?"

"We heard that she arrived at Juttah safely and that she is helping Elizabeth." Anna smiled, determined not to reveal her worry. "The most amazing thing has happened—Elizabeth is with child. I expect Mary will want to stay until the baby is born."

Joseph set the cheese aside, his mouth shifting just enough to bristle the beard on his cheek. "When . . . how long will that be?"

"You have built a fine house." Anna took a step back to better take in the strong frame that would soon be filled in with earthen bricks. "Mary will be so pleased."

Joseph grasped a beam propped against his father's courtyard wall. "There is still much work to do. I want to have it finished before Mary returns." He hesitated, then looked directly into Anna's eyes. "You didn't say when Elizabeth's baby will be born."

Anna drew a breath and struggled through an awkward moment. "In another month, I think."

"As long as that?" He nodded slowly. "I should get back to work."

"Joseph?"

He turned, a question in his eyes.

"Mary has never broken a promise," Anna said. "She will return, and before the wheat harvest."

Joseph glanced through a framed window toward the wheat fields, where the stalks were nearly knee-high. A smile replaced the uncertain expression she'd seen on his face earlier. "Thank you."

chapter thirteen

Days melted into weeks and weeks into months as Mary settled into her life as an expectant mother. Because of Elizabeth's advanced age, Mary was happy to tend the donkey, draw the water, and help with the meals. In return, Elizabeth taught her many things and never laughed or frowned at Mary's questions about what to expect in the months ahead.

As Elizabeth's time drew near, Mary noticed that her own belly had begun to swell. Three months had passed since the angel appeared in the olive grove, which meant her own child would be born in six months' time.

Would she be ready?

If not for Elizabeth and the other women who drew her into their intimate sorority, Mary would have been bewildered by her inexplicable queasiness around food, the tenderness in her breasts, the way she could feel overjoyed one moment and at the point of tears the next. Whenever a new manifestation of pregnancy caught her unaware, she would confide in Elizabeth, who rubbed her back and assured her that these quirks were not unusual among expectant women. These peculiarities—and others—would pass in time.

On a hot afternoon in Elizabeth's ninth month, Mary glanced at the cloudless sky and hurried from the well to her kinswoman's house.

That morning Elizabeth had complained of back pains, so several of the village women had been summoned to sit with her. One of the women was a midwife, and all of them had borne children.

By the time Mary entered the courtyard, she could hear Elizabeth's cries. She shouldered her way through the other women and knelt at her cousin's side. "Peace, dear cousin, and patience," she said, wiping sweat from Elizabeth's gray hairline. "You will soon hold your son in your arms."

The midwife crossed her arms. "Do not make rash promises—it could be a girl."

Mary exchanged a secret smile with her laboring kinswoman. "It is a boy. Now . . . is there nothing we can do to ease her pain?"

The woman squatted by Elizabeth's side. "You can rub her shoulders and give her water when she thirsts. The baby is ready. Won't be long now."

When Elizabeth relaxed as the pain of a contraction eased, the midwife prodded her. "Get up. Walk. Walk off the pain."

Elizabeth groaned and allowed herself to be pulled up. The other women, Mary noticed, had busied themselves with preparations for the infant—one was folding strips of swaddling cloth; another held a bowl of salt and a jar of oil.

Despite her concern about Elizabeth's well-being, Mary knew she ought to pay close attention. In a few months she, too, would be surrounded by women and urged on by a midwife. Yet even with experienced help, sometimes the process of childbirth went tragically wrong.

"Where is Zechariah?" Elizabeth said, pressing one hand to the small of her back. "The man is never around when I—oh!" She reached for Mary's arm. "The child," she hissed through clenched teeth, "is coming!"

"Sit," the midwife commanded, setting an odd-looking stool in the center of the room. "Sit now!"

Mary led Elizabeth to the wooden seat. Shaped like a half-moon, the birthing stool stood no higher than her knees.

Slowly, assisted by the other women, Elizabeth sank onto the stool while the midwife knelt in front of her.

"Now," the midwife commanded, opening her hands between Elizabeth's knees, "push!"

Elizabeth's face went red as she held her breath and squeezed Mary's hands. Mary felt her own limbs contract in sympathy as Elizabeth struggled against age and weariness to bring her promised son into the world.

From the corner of her eye, Mary saw a dark, wet head appear. A compact pair of shoulders followed; then a baby slid into the midwife's hands on a tide of blood and water.

"Elizabeth," the midwife crowed, her broad face creasing in a smile as she turned the wailing infant over. "You have given your husband a son!"

Mary stared in fascination at the tiny wet body, the pulsing umbilical cord, the strong fleshy legs. Though she had been at home when her sister-in-law gave birth, the men had kept her in the courtyard with them during Tirza's labor and delivery. Even if she had been allowed in the house, Mary knew she would not have been particularly interested in childbirth.

Now everything had changed.

One of the women took Elizabeth's baby and bathed him in a bowl of water, then dried him with a square of linen. While the midwife tended to Elizabeth and delivered the afterbirth, the other women rubbed the squalling child with oil and salt and wrapped his tiny limbs in swaddling clothes.

Mary swatted at a pair of buzzing flies, then smiled at the baby, who seemed uncomfortable being the center of so much attention. When the infant had been washed, salted, and swaddled, the midwife placed him in Elizabeth's arms.

Mary felt a pang of yearning as the perfect little boy rooted in search of his mother's life-sustaining breast. This child, this tiny one, would grow to be great in the eyes of God . . . and would prepare the way for her son.

The midwives offered a chorus of praise, and Mary laughed with delight to see the infant in her cousin's arms.

Eight days after the child's birth, the midwife, the village rabbi, and several friends joined the family for the baby's circumcision.

The rabbi took the infant and lifted him, then recited the traditional prayers: "Let his father rejoice in the issue of his loins and his mother in the fruit of her womb. May you always remember ADONAI our God, who always stands by his covenant, the commitment he made to a thousand generations."

One of the guests, a kinsman of Zechariah's, lifted a cup of wine. "And what name have you given him? The name of his father?"

Elizabeth smiled. "His name is John."

An older woman shook her head. "But there is no one in your family with that name." She looked at the rabbi. "Surely this cannot be Zechariah's wish. It is not done."

The midwife turned to Elizabeth. "Where has this name come from?"

"Where all names come from," Elizabeth answered. She nodded toward her husband. "Ask him."

The rabbi turned to Zechariah. "Honored friend, do you not wish for your son to carry your name?"

Zechariah's gaze caught and held his wife's, then shifted to Mary. With a confident smile on his lips, he gestured for a stylus and papyrus. When the instruments had been handed to him, with bold and confident strokes Zechariah wrote *His name is John.*

As the rabbi took the papyrus, Zechariah reached for his son and lifted him in his arms. "His name is John," he said, the sound of his voice rumbling through the house.

Tears of joy flowed over Elizabeth's pale cheeks, and Mary clapped in delight as the neighbors marveled.

Zechariah, his tongue now loosened, began to exalt the Lord with renewed fervor. "Praise ADONAI, the God of Isra'el, because he has visited his people and redeemed them. He has sent us a mighty Savior from the royal line of his servant David, just as he promised through his holy prophets long ago."

His gaze softened as he lowered the baby and held him in the crook of his arm. "And you, my little son, will be called the prophet of the Most High because you will prepare the way for the Lord. You will tell his people how to find salvation through forgiveness of their sins."

Elizabeth, with ribbons of tears trailing over her face, looked at Mary and whispered, "Amen."

With a heart too full for words, Mary looked out the window. The night shadows had gathered beneath a darkening sky, but one brilliant star sparkled against the black velvet horizon.

Two days later, Mary stood outside the house, her small traveling bag at her feet. Elizabeth and Zechariah stood inside the courtyard gate, both of them gazing at the infant in Mary's arms.

"You are certain this is what you are called to do?" Elizabeth asked, concern shining in her eyes. "To go home and marry this man? You know you are welcome to stay with us."

"This man was chosen for me," Mary answered. "If I run from him, I am denying my father's wish . . . and a daughter should obey her father just as she obeys ADONAI. Besides—" she returned Zechariah's smile—"being here, I have seen that a child will need a father. I hope this is ADONAI's will for my son."

Elizabeth's mouth curved with tenderness. "I will pray for you."

"Bless you, dearest cousin. Bless you and your child." Mary bent and brushed a kiss across the soft fuzz on the baby's head. "He is so precious."

"God is good," Elizabeth whispered, reaching for her son. "To you and to me."

Mary shifted the infant from her arms to her cousin's. " 'A mighty windstorm hit the mountain,'" she murmured, "'but ADONAI was not in the wind.' Nor in the earthquake. Nor in the fire."

She gazed at the child for one more moment, imprinting his tiny face upon her memory, then smiled. "'But after the fire, there came the sound of a gentle whisper.'"

She caught the priest's eye as she lifted her bag. "ADONAI often works in surprising ways, doesn't he?"

chapter fourteen

Firmly ensconced in a group of travelers headed for Galilee, Mary rejoiced to find herself in the company of more than a dozen women. She had nearly been overwhelmed with so many new names and faces when Zechariah introduced her to the group outside Jerusalem, but the women, all from one family, welcomed her with open arms. The men walked at the front and rear of the band, leaving their wives and mothers in the center to talk of matters and mysteries dear to women's hearts: husbands, children, and babies.

Few of her fellow travelers guessed the secret Mary carried, for her spacious tunic disguised the telltale bulge at her center.

But one woman, grayer and more stooped than the others, pulled Mary aside as they stopped to water the pack animals at a spot where a stream trickled through a wadi. "You have been away a long time?" the woman asked, a small smirk on her lips.

"Nearly four months." Mary lifted her hand to shade her eyes. "I heard my cousin was expecting a baby. I went to see if I could be of some help during her confinement."

The woman's smile broadened, revealing a missing front tooth. "And who will help you when your time comes?"

Mary glanced down, realizing for the first time that the rising wind had molded her tunic to her changing form. "I have a mother," she said quickly, embarrassed by the old woman's scrutiny. "And there are midwives in my village."

The old woman gripped her worn walking stick. "Good. The first child never wants to leave the womb; he will cause you the most pain."

Mary struggled to smile out of respect for her elders, though some perverse part of her wondered why other women felt compelled to share thoughts that brought more fear than comfort.

"God keep you," the woman said, hobbling away. "May ADONAI make you as fruitful as Rachel and Leah."

Mary's stomach churned as the old woman rejoined her daughters. As fruitful as Rachel and Leah? Only ADONAI knew if she would ever bear another child. As only he knew whether or not Joseph would welcome her into his home once he learned the secret she carried.

Because if the old woman had seen and understood, the truth would be obvious to those closest to her. She could not forestall the inevitable confrontation any longer.

Joseph and her family would have to be told . . . and she would have to bear the consequences of this most perilous blessing.

The wheat fields, which had been dark with promise when Mary left, rippled like a sea of gold as she and her companions climbed the road to Nazareth. The early morning sun bathed the mountainside village in dazzling light, generating a fierce nostalgia within her. Despite her anxieties, the sight of her beloved hometown quickened her pulse and sent a fountain of joy rising within her.

She walked past the olive grove and through the city gates, lingering only a moment as her fellow travelers exchanged greetings with the elders gathered there. After saying farewell to her new friends, Mary pulled her bag from a pack animal and slipped down the street that would lead her home.

She found her family gathered around a breakfast platter in the house. She embraced her mother and father, pinched her uncle's arm, bowed before her grandfather, and swung Hannah and Hodiya around until they squealed. After giving the girls affectionate kisses, she sank gratefully to the mat beside the cook fire. "How is everyone in Nazareth? I see the wheat is nearly ready to harvest."

"You have come back just in time," her mother answered, a grateful smile on her lips. "But I knew you would keep your promise."

Mary turned to her uncle. "When does the harvest begin?"

"After the Sabbath," he answered, grinning. "We must get the crop in before Herod realizes how richly ADONAI has blessed us."

Mary smiled at her uncle's wry comment, then eyed the breakfast of fruit, bread, and cheese. Her stomach clenched, ravenous for something besides dry bread and water. She glanced at the girls, who had gone to the courtyard to feed the goats. "Has everyone eaten?"

Her mother hugged her knees and rested her chin on her hand. "Go ahead, eat. You must be starving."

As Mary devoured a hunk of cheese, her mother sat across from her and watched with sharp eyes. "You were gone a long time."

Her mouth too full to speak, Mary nodded. After swallowing, she tried to explain. "I sent word by Miryam the weaver. Did she not give you my message?"

"She told us Elizabeth was expecting, so you had decided to stay until after the baby's birth."

Mary reached for a cup of water. After so many days in the sun and wind, her throat felt as dry as sand.

Her father stirred uneasily. "The child was safely born?"

"Yes—Elizabeth has a son. He is a lovely boy and a special child." Mary hesitated, not certain how she should broach the subject of the child's miraculous birth.

"We heard other things about Elizabeth," her father went on. "We heard about Zechariah . . . and an angel."

Mary exhaled in relief, grateful that at least part of her news wouldn't be a complete surprise. "Zechariah stunned many in Juttah and Jerusalem with his story. Many months ago, an angel told him he would have a son who would be great in the eyes of God. Zechariah and Elizabeth are to raise their son as a Nazarite because he will prepare the way for the One who is to come."

"One who is to . . ." Her mother's eyes narrowed. "Zechariah believed this tale?"

"Not at first," Mary admitted, plucking a handful of grapes from the stem. "That's why the angel struck him dumb. Not until Zechariah named the child at the circumcision could he speak again."

"He may wish he'd held his tongue even then." Her mother's dark gaze flew to her husband's face. "If he spreads talk of a Messiah, there will be trouble."

Mary's nerves tensed. "Why trouble? Have we not been waiting for the Messiah?"

"Think about it, Mary." Her father's voice sharpened. "If you were ADONAI, would you send the Messiah into a world like this? One man cannot defeat Herod *and* Rome." He shook his head. "HaShem will send our deliverer, but not, I fear, in my lifetime."

Aaron shrugged. "Who are we to tell ADONAI what he should do? If Zechariah saw an angel, who are we to question him? He is a righteous man. In any case, time will reveal the truth of his words."

Mary stopped eating, her hand in midair. Surely there could be no better time than this moment. All she had to do was say that she'd seen an angel too; in fact, she'd seen Gabriel, the same messenger who appeared to Zechariah. Then she could say *another* special child would be born, one whose arrival had been foretold through the ages. . . .

Her mother's brow wrinkled as something moved in her eyes. "Did Elizabeth not give you food for your journey? I have never seen you stuff yourself like—"

Without warning, her dark gaze blazed into Mary's with an extraordinary expression of alarm. As swift as a cat, her mother leaned across the space between them, her hand reaching for the small, warm mound that had sprouted beneath Mary's ribs. Her mother's face twisted when she touched the growing womb. Without a word, she sank back to her mat, her eyes wide and vacant.

Aware that something significant and disturbing had passed between the women, Mary's uncle lifted a brow and looked from his niece to his sister-in-law.

Filming on the Nazareth set outside Matera, Italy, Keisha Castle-Hughes (Mary) takes a break from acting to substitute for our assistant camera in working the clapboard. The scene she's marking is when Joseph brings the donkey back from the tax collectors and gives it to Mary.

Oscar Isaac (Joseph) and director Catherine Hardwicke review scenes outside Joseph's house.

Director Catherine Hardwicke and first assistant director Justin Muller survey the city of Matera as it stands in for Jerusalem. The green screen above the archway has been put in place so they can matte paint the rest of the city to look older and more realistic to what Jerusalem would have been like at the time of Christ's birth.

Some of the extras from the Jerusalem crosses day of filming play with their own cameras as the still photographer takes a snapshot of them.

One of the local Moroccan men was taught how to handle snakes by his father, and he became our on-set snake handler. The scene being shot is of Mary falling off the donkey into the river after the donkey is frightened by a snake.

Zechariah writes upon a scroll inside his home.

The camera department rigs the scene in which Mary falls off the donkey and into the river after being chased by the snake. Left to right: Marco Maggi, Emiliano Topai, Guilio

Catherine Hardwicke and Stanley Townsend (Zechariah) rehearse the scene inside the Temple in which Zechariah doubts the words of the angel Gabriel and is struck dumb.

During the filming in Italy, screenwriter Mike Rich (center) dropped in for a couple of days to see his writing come to life. On this particular day, Keisha, Mike, and Oscar were able to spend some time together during a break from filming the scenes in which Mary and Joseph come down the hillside just outside of Nazareth on the donkey and come upon a group of shepherds.

Our hawk wrangler sends the bird in flight as a test run for the pivotal angel Gabriel scene.

A set production assistant in Morocco loads Mary's and Joseph's wet costumes into a dryer brought down from base camp and set up on the mountainside. During the sequence in which Mary falls in the river, the action had to be filmed multiple times and each time Mary and Joseph had to be wearing dry costumes. So we trucked industrial

Director Catherine Hardwicke relaxes with the Nazareth townspeople.

Producers Wyck Godfrey and Marty Bowen discuss a scene.

Yvonne Scio, playing a Jerusalem street merchant, is framed by Steadicam operator George Billinger. As filming took place in Italy, hundreds of extras were brought in to fill some of the smaller roles, but for the role of Vashti, the ribbon seller, Italian TV personality Yvonne Scio was selected for her exotic beauty.

One of our extras from the Jerusalem set in traditional clothing.

Catherine Hardwicke (left of center in white shirt) directs the props department working on the crosses on the hills outside Jerusalem (Matera).

First assistant director Justin Muller readies a baby sheep to run in front of the camera during the sequence in which the angel Gabriel appears to the elder shepherd and tells him about the Christ child.

Wyck Godfrey, Marty Bowen, and visual effects supervisor Theresa Rygiel stand on the mountains outside Matera and watch over the scenes of soldiers charging down the hill toward Bethlehem to execute Herod's command to "slaughter the innocents."

Ciarán Hinds (King Herod) and Catherine Hardwicke discuss a scene set in Jerusalem

Catherine Hardwicke gives direction to Keisha Castle-Hughes (sitting atop Gilda, the donkey) with Oscar Isaac at the entrance to Bethlehem.

Oscar Isaac and Keisha Castle-Hughes walk up the streets of Matera, Italy.
Catherine Hardwicke directs from the right side (green shirt).

The final night of filming in Italy is capped off by a cast and crew shot under the
bright lights of the Bethlehem set with everyone sitting in and around the manger.
The Nativity Story's own Nativity scene.

"Aaron," her mother said, her voice empty and flat, "if you have finished, why don't you take the girls to the fields."

Mary lowered her head lest Aaron see the blush heating her cheekbones. On any other day her teasing uncle would have tried to discover the source of her discomfort, but the expression on her mother's face allowed no room for jesting.

Aaron stood, reached for his staff, and did not even glance at Mary before calling his daughters and leaving the house.

When Mary sat alone with her parents and grandfather, her mother spoke again. "Your daughter—" her gaze moved to her husband's face—"is with child."

Neither man spoke, though Grandfather Avram's lower lip began to tremble.

Mary closed her eyes, for even in the heavy silence, the house rang with unspoken accusations. She drew a deep breath, then raised her head and met her father's astounded gaze. "I know what you must be thinking, but I have broken no vow."

Her mother folded her arms. "Is the child Joseph's?"

Mary averted her eyes, unable to answer. How could she explain when her mother automatically assumed the worst?

"If the child is not Joseph's," her mother continued in a voice like chilled steel, "then you have broken *every* vow."

Mary lifted her chin. "I must ask you to have faith."

Her father clenched his hand. "Why should we have faith in you? Do you know how much disgrace you have brought upon yourself? upon Joseph?" A surge of anguish roughened his voice. "The Law required you to remain pure until you moved into his house."

Mary lifted her chin and forced herself to meet her father's piercing gaze. "I have honored the Law."

Her mother drew in a quick breath, then groaned. "Was it one of Herod's soldiers? one of the Romans? someone on the journey to Juttah?"

Mary shook her head. "I have asked you to have faith—"

"How can you keep saying that? Wake up, Mary—women have been put to death for this!" Her father propped his elbow on his knee, then abruptly lowered his arm and leaned toward his daughter. "You should have stayed at Elizabeth's house. You could have birthed the child there, away from the people of your village—"

"I am not following Elizabeth's will in this. I am following . . . the will of ADONAI. An angel appeared to me and told me I would bear a child who will be called the Son of God."

Her parents' faces went blank with shock; then her mother's stunned expression dissolved into lines of grief. "An angel told you this." Disbelief echoed in her voice. "That you would bear the Son of God."

"The angel told me Elizabeth was pregnant, and she had a baby. It was a miracle. You know it was—"

"Elizabeth had a husband!" The words came out as a vehement hiss.

Mary shrank from the sound and lowered her head, wishing she could draw herself up beneath her veil and not come out.

After a long moment, her father spoke. "You sound very sure of yourself, Mary, but men are not forgiving. Joseph is a good man, but this will be too much for him to bear." He shook his head and rose from the floor. "Trust me, Daughter. No man I know could accept this. I don't know how we're supposed to tell Joseph—"

"You don't have to tell him. I'm going to see him today. I'll tell him everything."

Mary hadn't planned on paying Joseph a visit so soon, but now she knew she had no choice.

chapter fifteen

In the house he had built with his hands and heart, Joseph sat in stunned silence, unable to believe the story his betrothed had just told him. "I have waited so long for your return, Mary." He studied her face, still sweet, still pure. "Now you are here and you tell me that you—"

"Whatever you decide, I will understand." She nodded as if to emphasize her point. "You are a righteous man, and I know this is hard news to accept. But, Joseph, you must believe I have done nothing wrong. I am betrothed to you, I have been faithful to you, and I have done everything the Law has asked of me." She looked down and stared at her hands. "That is all I can say."

Silence fell between them, an absence of sound that felt like a physical barrier. Joseph looked at the woman for whom he had been waiting, the woman for whom he had been saving himself. . . .

How had this madness come about?

He was on the verge of dismissing her out of sheer bewilderment when some small remnant of outrage trickled out of him. "Do you know the reason I chose you, Mary? Why I waited so many years to approach your father?"

She lifted her head but did not speak.

"They told me you were a young woman of great virtue." He heard derision in his voice, but he couldn't help himself. "I have spent my life seeking honor. I have sought righteousness in a time when righteousness was not easy to find. But how am I to answer you? If I claim the child is mine, I will be lying. I will have broken God's law."

Mary closed her eyes. "I would never ask you to lie."

"If I say the child is *not* mine," Joseph continued, "they will ask what I want to do with you. If I accuse you of this—this *sin* . . ." He looked at her, hoping she would supply the answer to this terrible dilemma, but she only stared at the ground, waiting to hear his decision.

Sometimes the role of leadership chafed against his shoulders.

"There is a purpose for this child," Mary answered, her voice faint, "greater than my fear of what people may do to me."

Her calm, her utter unconcern, maddened and baffled him. For an instant anger rose in his gut, fierce and strong. He swiped at a wooden bowl on his workbench, sending it spinning across the room.

Mary winced.

And at this small sign of her vulnerability, his anger faded as quickly as it had arisen. How could such a woman be unfaithful? In her eyes he saw neither guile nor disloyalty. Only faithfulness. Truth. And an utter willingness to accept whatever he decided . . . even if he decided she deserved death.

He could not subject such a woman to scorn.

"I will make no public accusation," he finally said, slumping under the weight of his words. "Without that, there will be no trial."

She gave him a brief, distracted glance and attempted to smile. "But . . . you will not take me as your wife?"

He did not know how to answer.

Mary nodded as color crept up from her neck. "You have shown me great mercy, Joseph. For that I will always be grateful."

She rose from her seat and left him alone.

Joseph didn't know how long he sat at the table after Mary left. He was dimly aware of lengthening shadows, of his stomach rumbling, of approaching darkness. Across the street, his neighbors lit their lamps, but he couldn't summon the will or the energy to light his nearly finished house.

This was supposed to be the home where he would rejoice with his bride, where they would raise a family. Joseph had cut every beam and placed every brick with thoughts of children at his knees—boys who would study Torah and girls who would work alongside their beautiful mother.

He had labored and planned and dreamed . . . only to discover that his virtuous bride carried a shameful secret. A child, not his.

She'd told him of the angel, but he'd heard a similar tale about her cousin Elizabeth. Mary must have borrowed the story and embellished it to hide her shame. Perhaps she truly believed it. In his years he had heard rumors of unfortunate girls who were violated and so upset that a sort of madness ensued. They could not remember the attack or name the man who had stolen their purity. Perhaps Mary had been attacked on the road to Juttah; perhaps she was not completely in her right mind.

He sighed, releasing a tide of weariness. He could not make a decision tonight. He wanted nothing more than to lie down and lose himself in forgetfulness, shoving aside the unfortunate moment when Mary had appeared at his threshold and shared her terrible confession.

He lay down on the straw mattress—one he had stuffed thinking of his bride—closed his eyes, and willed himself to enter oblivion. Unconsciousness came slowly, but sleep finally nudged itself into his fitful thoughts and carried his worries away. . . .

But not far enough. From the doorway of his house he saw Mary walking down the narrow, twisting street, a water vessel on her hip. Two of the devout elders watched her approach, then leaned in to whisper as she walked by. She walked past the olive press, where other men looked at her and whispered to their neighbors.

Undoubtedly aware of her neighbors' scorn, Mary quickened her pace, water sloshing from her jug as she hurried over the cobblestones.

One of the men at the olive press picked up a stone and threw it at her retreating figure, hitting her squarely in the back.

Joseph inhaled a hard breath and stepped into the street in time to see others bend to pick up rocks.

Mary set down her water jug and began to run, and the villagers ran after her, their hands clenched around rocks and stones intended to do damage.

As Joseph followed the crowd, the sound of Joaquim's voice came back on a tide of memory: *"But you shall consider him your husband . . . in all manner except that which leads to children."*

Joseph's own voice, heavy with love: *"I promise to please, honor, nourish, and care for you, as is the manner of the men of Isra'el."*

Her mother's affirmation: *"Mary has never broken a promise."*

He rounded a corner and saw another stone fly, missing Mary by inches.

She stopped, whirling in the street to face her accusers. "But I have done nothing wrong!"

A shouted accusation, another protest of innocence, then a stone struck her brow. As a trickle of blood flowed, a storm of rocks flew toward her, striking her hands, her arms, her swollen stomach.

A man standing on the corner picked up a rock, ran his thumb over a sharp edge, and offered the stone to Joseph.

Joseph backed away as his gut twisted. He could not watch this. He turned away, leaving Mary to her fate.

But a man blocked the road. A man standing alone, unaffected by the noise, the tumult, the emotion. He looked at Joseph with eyes that gleamed with the light of a dozen stars and seemed capable of reading the intent of a human heart. "Joseph, son of David."

Joseph felt his knees turn to water. This was no resident of Nazareth. Men like this did not live among mortals.

"Joseph, son of David," the glowing visitor repeated, a look of eagerness in his eyes, "do not be afraid to go ahead with your marriage to Mary, for the child within her has been conceived by the Holy Spirit. . . ."

Awestruck, Joseph listened.

The sound of a rising wind roused Joseph from slumber. He sat up in the darkness, awareness settling over him like a warm cloak.

He was lying in the house he was supposed to share with Mary. He was *home*.

He rolled off the mattress and walked to the doorway, open to the warm night beyond. Around him, past the silvered courtyard and the narrow street, Nazareth slept under a starlit sky.

Did any of his friends and acquaintances know of the miracle among them? Mary knew. He knew. Perhaps her parents had realized the truth by now.

The prophets and sages realized the truth long ago. Filled with the Spirit of God, they looked into the future and predicted these astounding events.

Isaiah wrote of the coming miracle . . . and Joseph had been chosen to witness the prophecy's fulfillment: "Look! The virgin will conceive a child! She will give birth to a son and will call him Immanuel—'God is with us.'"

Joseph looked up at the heavens, where a single star outshone all the others.

Joseph rose early the next morning, washed his face and hands, and pulled a new cloak over his shoulders. According to custom, he should have friends go with him to the bride's house, but he wanted to make this journey alone.

He strode through the streets with long steps, then paused in the northeast corner of the city. Mary stood by the well, a pitcher on her hip, but none of the other women had ventured near her. Three or four had gathered several feet away, their faces animated as they buzzed over some secret.

The scene, so like his dream, sent a flicker of apprehension coursing through his veins.

Unaware of Joseph's presence, Mary knelt to talk to a little girl, whose face brightened at the unexpected attention. Joseph leaned against a wall, content to watch, until the girl's mother stepped out of the other women's circle and drew her daughter away.

Gossip, he realized, traveled like the wind.

When Mary's face fell, Joseph felt an instant's squeezing hurt. He would have walked over to comfort her, but he didn't want to give the women anything else to talk about.

The news he'd come to bring this morning was for Mary alone.

He lingered in the shadows until she filled her water jug and moved away. He followed, remaining only a few steps behind, until she stopped to undo the latch on her father's courtyard gate. Then he pitched his words to reach Mary's ear and not a breath beyond. "And you shall call his name . . . Jesus, salvation of Yahweh."

She turned, startled.

His eyes clung to hers, analyzing her reaction. "For he will save his people from their sins."

Mary swiped tears from her cheeks, then peered up at him through tear-clotted lashes. "You . . . know?"

Joseph stepped closer. "The child will need a father."

"Yes."

"I will declare him as my own."

Mary smiled as fresh tears welled within her eyes. "The villagers . . . they may not believe anything we say. They may never accept the truth."

"I cannot worry about pleasing other people. Not now." He extended his hand. "You are my legal wife. I am your husband. That is all anyone needs to know."

"And . . . as to the future?"

"Our home is nearly finished, Mary. All it lacks is a few nails, a shelf or two . . . and a bride." He lowered his head until the world consisted of nothing but her eyes. "I'm asking you to come home with me, Mary. Today you shall become my wife."

chapter sixteen

Melchior spread the celestial maps on the low table at the center of the room and lowered his aging limbs to a cushion. "Take a look, my friends, and tell me if you see any significance in these charts."

Balthasar leaned forward to study the stellar representations of the Lion, the Virgin, and the Bear. He turned his face toward the sliver of night sky visible through the open window. "I would love to provide a definite answer for you, Melchior, but the star charts cannot explain the mystery that keeps you awake at night."

"It is definitely not a comet." Melchior followed Balthasar's gaze. The unidentified star hung in the western sky, taunting them with its light and its mystery. "It moves but not quickly."

Gaspar lifted the scroll in his hands. "Do you still believe the star could be linked to the prophecy of Balaam?"

Melchior nodded. "I do. The Hebrew prophet Jeremiah wrote that the true God would place a righteous Branch on David's throne in Jerusalem. Isaiah proclaimed that out of the stump of David's family, a shoot would grow—a Branch bearing fruit from the old root."

Gaspar stroked his oiled beard. "Perhaps Balaam spoke of Israel's David."

"Mighty David won many victories," Melchior replied, "but he did not completely annihilate the enemies of Israel. No, I believe

Balaam spoke of an altogether different king. A ruler who will be born in Judea."

Balthasar's eyes widened. "So this new king will be more powerful than David?"

Melchior returned his attention to the map of the heavens. "He is called the Lion of Judah, so it would appear so."

Balthasar picked up his brass astrolabe and twirled the dial. "Indeed. The words of the prophets are being fulfilled . . . if they have not been fulfilled already."

Melchior focused his attention on the star chart. The aged king who currently sat on Israel's throne was an Edomite, not a Jew, so the king he sought could not be of Herod's lineage. Yet Herod had ruled with Rome's permission and authority for years . . . and how could anyone challenge Rome?

A wry smile appeared in the thicket of Gaspar's curled beard. "Do my eyes deceive me? You are uncertain, Melchior."

"I am." Melchior turned the map, glanced at the sky again, and sighed. "We have observed the heavens and studied the prophecies for several months now. We have watched a strange star that glows with uncommon brightness. But we have no convincing proof of a new king."

He reached for a stylus, dipped it in ink, and marked the mysterious star's current location on the map. "If the true God is proclaiming the birth of the Jews' promised Messiah . . . he is doing so quietly."

Without warning, Balthasar dropped his astrolabe, the instrument hitting the stone floor with a ringing clang. "How could I have been so blind?"

Melchior lifted a brow. "What?"

"I've been thinking of numbers and positions; I should have been thinking of words and meanings."

Melchior's mind whirled at the bizarre response. "Perhaps you'd better explain."

Balthasar scooted closer to the table where Melchior had spread the star chart. "Look, look here. We first became aware of the mystery when Venus and Jupiter conjoined; do you remember? But a few days later, notice which two stars were in conjunction." He grabbed his armillary sphere, adjusted the colures, and handed the sphere to Melchior. "Now do you see?"

Melchior studied the instrument. "I see Venus joined with Mercury. Four months ago."

Balthasar grinned as happily as a poor man who'd just discovered a bag of gold. "Venus is the fertile mother. Mercury is the messenger of God. Four months ago, the messenger visited the mother."

Melchior stared, tongue-tied, at the sphere in his hand.

"That's interesting," Gaspar called from his cushion, "but it could also be a coincidence. Mercury often conjoins with Venus—"

"But look at this." Balthasar took the armillary sphere and set it in its stand, positioning the sun in the proper astrological house for whatever date he had in mind. "Your mystery star, Melchior, is not a true mystery. Now I see its track. It is Sharu, the star the Romans call Regulus."

Melchior sat back, startled to hear the word for *king* in two languages. "Why didn't I recognize it?"

"Because it is brighter than usual. And because you have never seen Jupiter hovering over it. A close Jupiter-Venus-Sharu conjunction will not happen again in our lifetimes . . . no, not until our grandchildren's children have gone to their graves, if then."

Melchior stared at the star chart as Balthasar continued. "In the coming months, three times Jupiter will conjoin with Sharu in the constellation of the Lion. On all three occasions, Jupiter, the father of kings, will circle above Sharu, the little king, while Sharu appears between the lion's feet."

Melchior closed his eyes as an old Hebrew prophecy surfaced in a shiver of vivid recollection: *The scepter will not pass from Judah, nor the ruler's staff from between his legs, until he comes . . .*"

Venus, Jupiter, Sharu.

Mother, Father, King.

The Lion of Judah.

Abruptly, he strode out of the chamber.

Melchior had just lifted the lid of his trunk when he heard the shuffling steps of his companions. For a moment Balthasar and Gaspar stood at his threshold and stared wordlessly. Balthasar pressed his hand to his chest. "Melchior, my esteemed friend . . . what are you doing?"

"Packing."

"May I ask why?"

"Because——" he tossed a robe into the chest and grinned at his former student—"I am going to greet the Lion of Judah. Do you think I would miss the opportunity of a lifetime?"

Gaspar stepped forward. "Surely it would be more advantageous for you to take a *spiritual* journey, Melchior. We could summon a Hebrew holy man or find a prophet who could satisfy your curiosity."

Melchior ignored the suggestion and reached for a length of silk. He would need something light to cover his head on the journey, something to protect him from the desert sun.

Balthasar cleared his throat. "You truly wish to travel to the land of Judea?"

"No." Melchior straightened, amused by the swift look of relief that crossed their faces. "I think we should all go."

Gaspar and Balthasar glanced at each other; then Gaspar broke the silence. "Melchior, the land you speak of is far away. We know nothing of the dangers we may find . . . and who would believe our reason for the journey? People will laugh if we tell them we are following a star."

As Gaspar released a prolonged and artificial chuckle, Melchior looked at Balthasar. "Surely *you* will join me."

The astronomer blinked. "We can track the star from here."

"I don't want to see the star. I want to see what the star portends. I want to *follow* the star, not track it."

"Yes, well. To follow the star, I would need my charts, my instruments——"

"Then take them." Melchior threw a silk pillow into his trunk.

"B-but," Balthasar sputtered, "what about my cushions, my pillows . . . and my bed? I have refined tastes, Melchior; I have grown accustomed to the very best."

"I, too, enjoy our comforts," Gaspar echoed. "I need my food—my dates, my nuts, my spices. What about my *wine*, Melchior?"

Melchior knelt before another trunk, one protected by a lock. His most precious possessions lay within, the only objects he owned that might be appropriate gifts for a king.

He contemplated the lock for a moment, then glanced over his shoulder, surprised to find his companions still waiting. "Are you so reluctant to discover what God has revealed? If we need to carry a pack camel, consider it done. But join me. Both of you."

He paused, waiting for a response, and when he turned again Gaspar was kneading a frown line between his brows.

"Only one pack camel?" he asked.

chapter seventeen

A dry wind rattled over the barren wheat field, stripped now of its harvest. Mary used the corner of her veil to wipe a trickle of perspiration from her brow, then shifted the bag on her shoulder and focused her attention on the shorn stalks. The Law commanded harvesters to leave any grain that might fall for the poor, but this field had been thoroughly gleaned.

Her mouth watered at the thought of the breakfast her mother would have spread out that morning: cheese and plump figs, grapes, and wheat bread. . . .

Mary'd had to make adjustments since arriving at Joseph's house. Since he was not a farmer and had no lands outside the village, she had to either buy or glean whatever they ate. The only livestock her husband owned was a solitary donkey, so Mary would not have milk or cheese unless she bought it or saved enough to buy a goat.

She did not regret her decision to marry Joseph, but living with him, she'd come to realize, meant carving out a life completely unlike her mother's. Mary had become the wife of a tradesman, so unless she learned to bargain and barter, her pretty, well-constructed house might remain empty.

She tucked her bag securely under her arm and left the shorn wheat field, following the beaten path that led to the vineyard. The round grapes were juicy and ready for harvest, and most of the villagers were busy among the rows. Perhaps some of them would drop a stem for her to pick up.

The sound of voices reached her long before she crested the hill and saw the long lines of vines quilting the earth. She heard girls calling to one another, their light voices like careless sparrows chattering on a limb.

When she saw Rebecca and Naomi filling their baskets, she threaded her way through the supports and walked to the end of the row. She waited, hoping her friends would greet her. Rebecca glanced up but quickly averted her gaze. Mary thought she saw Rebecca's lips moving as she whispered something to Naomi, who worked the other side of the vines.

"Hello?" Mary called. "How goes the harvest?"

She paused, but neither girl lifted her head. After a long moment, Mary turned away, a flash of loneliness stabbing at her as she walked back to the village.

So . . . her friends wanted nothing to do with her. And something told her their diffidence sprang from more than disappointment in not being invited to her wedding.

That night, as Mary spread figs, bread, and a block of her mother's cheese on a platter for Joseph's dinner, she shut her eyes and allowed herself to revisit the wedding she had always imagined.

In her dreams her promised husband came to her father's house with his friends, his father, and his family. He pretended to surprise her, but because she and her bridesmaids had been forewarned, they'd spent all day preparing for his arrival. Eager to look her best, Mary dressed in a new tunic, a fine mantle, and a headdress of gold coins. A veil of the sheerest silk, through which her husband could see her tears of happiness, covered her head as the bridegroom took her hand and led her to his house for the wedding feast.

At the home of her betrothed, she stood with him under the wedding canopy while a rabbi recited the traditional blessing: "'Our sister, may you increase to thousands upon thousands; may your offspring possess the gates of their enemies.'" She and her groom then led dozens of wedding guests to a rich banquet, where everyone ate and drank the finest food and wine to celebrate the couple's happiness.

Afterward, two friends of the groom escorted her and her husband to the bridal chamber. She would have gone with her hair uncovered, freely flowing down her back for her husband to exclaim over its beauty. . . .

Mary slid her thumb across the platter, then yelped as a splinter entered her flesh. She brought her thumb to her mouth and bit it, hoping the pain would overshadow her longing for a dream that had been exchanged for something else.

Why was she allowing herself to become distracted with daydreams? Her actual wedding, while nothing like the event of her dreams, had been happy enough. Joseph came to her father's house alone, he caught her by surprise, and she wore a simple workday tunic. But before leaving her home, she paused for her parents' blessing and exchanged her dusty head covering for the white veil Joseph had given her.

He had taken her hand and led her through the slanting streets of Nazareth, walking with a calm and deliberate step as if daring anyone to object. At the threshold of his courtyard—her courtyard now—he placed his hand under her chin and lifted her face until she looked directly into his eyes. "I will honor you and the gift you carry," he whispered in a ragged voice. "You need not fear me, Mary. I will not claim my rights as a husband until after the babe is born."

She nodded, her heart welling with gratitude. She had not worn a headdress of gold coins at her wedding, but she had worn tears of happiness.

It was enough.

chapter eighteen

Melchior placed his foot upon the foreleg of his kneeling camel and swung himself into the saddle. The animal blew gustily and turned her head, blinking her long lashes.

"Yes, O camel of fleet feet." Melchior picked up the reins. "It is time to depart. No more packing, no more waiting."

Behind him, Balthasar sat upon a camel that carried nearly double the amount of saddlebags and waterskins. Two armed servants sat on dromedaries at the head of the line—not even Melchior would risk heading into unfamiliar territory without the support of a pair of good swordsmen.

He glanced behind them. No sign of Gaspar. Apparently the man cared more for his creature comforts than for a cosmic king.

"Are you ready, then?" Melchior called.

Balthasar nodded and kicked his mount. "Let's be off."

The camels rose in their slow, stately way, and Melchior clung to the saddle as his beast tipped him forward, then back. "Let's be off," he called to the servant at the front of the procession. "Let us cover as much ground as possible in the cool of the day."

The leader nodded and urged his mount forward.

Melchior drew his legs up as far as he could and wished he'd put another blanket atop the saddle. By the end of this day's journey, his bones would appreciate the extra padding.

They had traveled little more than an hour when Balthasar shouted for his attention. "Look! Behind us!"

Melchior turned in the saddle. Through the cloud of dust a pair of camels came forward at a trot, their heads bobbing to the rhythm of their feet. A single rider held his reins in one hand and waved a white cloth with the other.

Melchior felt a smile crack his sun-dried face.

Gaspar. Leading an extra pack camel.

chapter nineteen

As the ninth day of Tishri drew to a close, every citizen of Nazareth feasted with what God had provided during the harvests, then lit their lamps and dressed in white. Because the festival of Yom Kippur commenced with the sunset, the sons and daughters of Isra'el went to the synagogue, where they would hear the story of Jonah, the man who learned that he could not escape God's judgment.

From her window, Mary drew her cloak about her and watched her friends pass on their way to the synagogue. Naomi and Rebecca walked by, followed by Ruth and her gaggle of children. None of them even looked in Mary's direction.

She dressed in white too and waited for Joseph to finish washing so he could accompany her to the synagogue. As she listened to the sound of her husband splashing in the basin, her thoughts drifted toward the Temple in Jerusalem, where at the coming sunrise the high priest would ceremonially wash his hands and feet ten times. Dressed in his golden robes, he would offer the morning sacrifice before going again to the bathhouse, where he would wash and dress in garments of spotless white linen.

This time he would step outside and place his hand on the head of the bull intended for sacrifice. After confessing his sin, the priest would move to two identical goats tethered on the eastern side of the altar. He would reach into an urn and shuffle two golden tablets that would determine which of the goats would be sacrificed and which would be the scapegoat.

The priest would draw out the tablets, one with his right hand and one with his left. Then he would place his hands upon the goats' heads. The sacrificial animal would be led to the altar while the priest tied a red sash on the horns of the scapegoat.

Mary shivered as she recalled the one time she had witnessed the ceremony. The unfortunate scapegoat stood before the waiting congregation while the sacrificial animal was slain upon the altar. The scapegoat who bore the sins of the people could not be driven out until after the blood had been shed.

After the sacrificial goat had been killed and his blood sprinkled on the altar, a goat handler took the crimson sash from the scapegoat's horns, tore it in two, and retied one half to the animal's horns. As the people chanted, "Hurry and go," the handler led the animal through the Temple gate. Dozens of willing hands escorted the beast from point to point until the scapegoat reached a cliff outside the city. There, Mary knew, the goat would be pushed off the cliff and into a ravine. Like the sins of Isra'el, the scapegoat would be seen no more.

For the last several months in her beloved hometown, Mary had felt about as welcome as the scapegoat.

chapter twenty

Flushed with satisfaction after a good meal, Herod stood on a rampart of his palace, placed his hand on his stomach, and allowed himself the luxury of a public belch.

To his credit, Tero didn't even flinch.

"Look there." Herod gestured to the bustling Jerusalem market below. "My capital has become the marketplace of the world, a venue where citizens can buy cattle, ironware, wool, or fish, while their wives can find anything from a false tooth to a Persian shawl. But does Caesar come here to view my accomplishment? No. He remains in Rome and sends messages. Many messages." He lowered his voice to a disloyal whisper. "I've had it with his messages, Tero. His last said whereas of old he had used me as his friend, he would now use me as his subject."

Herod paced along the walls of the rampart, his hands clasped behind his back. "Rome is now requesting a census. Caesar wants to number the chickens in his henhouse, so each man is to return to the place of his birth and be counted."

The chief counselor bowed and touched his breast. "Excuse me, Excellency, but such an order may lead to further unrest. If we command already agitated people to leave their homes—"

"It is the will of Caesar." Herod shifted his gaze to the people milling in the marketplace below. The fools. They ran to and fro like ants, never knowing what pains he took for them, the worries he willingly bore on their behalf. He alone stood between them and Rome; he prevented the mighty eagle from plucking them bare. And how did they repay him for his effort? With ingratitude. And rebellion.

"My father—" he hesitated, disturbed by the memory—"my father lost his life because he failed to see the threats mounting against him. Threats that rose from the people he ruled."

Tero tilted his head, either unable or unwilling to offer a comment.

Herod blew out a breath. "This talk of rebellion—" he gestured to the Hebrews below—"how much of it rests in their hope for a new king?"

Tero could not escape a direct question. He closed his eyes as if formulating an answer, then looked up and showed his teeth in an expression that was not a smile. "The people have long believed a king will rise to save them . . . a man foretold by their prophets. They fail to see that you, their true king, are working hard for their good."

Herod ignored the flattery. "I am told they are looking for a Messiah who will follow in the footsteps of David . . . and be descended from the same lineage." He stared hard at the people, then spoke without turning to his counselor. "You have heard, haven't you, about my elder brother?" He heard the sound of sudden shuffling.

"I have heard many things about your noble family, Excellency. About your brother in particular—"

"He was a great man. At our father's wish, we governed together—Phasael ruled over Judea while I ruled Galilee. By treachery my brother was captured during the Parthian Wars . . . and died. For forty years, I have missed him."

Tero cleared his throat. "I have heard he was an exceptional soldier."

"He was great"—Herod turned—"because he did what had to be done without flinching. When captured by the enemy, he killed himself by bashing his head against the prison's stone wall. Death before dishonor, Tero. That is what Phasael believed; by that code he lived and died."

Herod braced his hands on the low wall. "Many times I ask

myself: What would Phasael do about this? about that? What would he do if he ruled these prickly people who refused to be properly governed? He would . . . set a trap for usurpers."

He straightened and crossed his arms as a new thought occurred. Rome had commanded a census, but a benefit might yet be derived from this nuisance.

"Tero—" he glanced over his shoulder—"the Hebrew prophets said this Messiah King would rise from the house of David, did they not?"

Tero blinked, then smiled in a quick curve of his lips. "That is my understanding, yes."

"And David ruled from Jerusalem." Herod pressed his fingertips to his temple as his thoughts whirled. This was delicious, too perfect. "So the census will bring any would-be kings . . . to us."

He lowered his hand and gave his counselor a sly smile. "Have your soldiers and spies keep watch for a man returning to Jerusalem. A man of power. A man the people will follow."

Tero swallowed hard, his wary gray eyes occupying most of the available space in his thin face. "And if we find such a man?"

Herod paused. "You have been with me a long time, Counselor. If you find anyone claiming to know of or be this Messiah, I trust you will live up to my brother's example and do what must be done."

chapter twenty-one

"Anna?"

Mary pushed herself up from the woven mat as Ruth's voice drifted from the courtyard. The baby lay heavy upon her these days, occasionally kicking at her spine and punching at her ribs.

With a hand pressed to the small of her back, she shuffled to the courtyard gate. "Mother is not here," she called, giving Ruth what she hoped was a pleasing smile. "I came over to watch the girls, and she told me you'd be coming by. I have the block of cheese you wanted."

Ruth's smile faded the moment Mary appeared in the doorway, but at least she didn't turn and walk away. Neither did she step into the courtyard, Mary noticed, but lingered on the street as if Mary were an outcast or a Gentile.

Mary lifted the cloth-covered cheese from the basket where it waited, then crossed the courtyard and delivered it to Ruth.

With the thinnest of smiles, Ruth dropped a coin onto Mary's palm.

"Thank you."

Ruth nodded and walked away.

Mary leaned against the gatepost and sighed as she dropped one hand to the mound of her belly. She had been honored when Gabriel told her she would bear a son . . . but she had not realized how much the honor would cost.

She turned, about to go back into the shade of the house, but a new sound joined the sigh of the palm branches overhead—the faint rip and roar of an agitated crowd. She hesitated at the courtyard gate and looked toward the town center. Something must have happened; perhaps someone had been hurt . . . Joseph?

Alarmed, she drew her veil from a peg on the wall, told her cousins not to leave the house, and slipped into the street.

At the market in the center of town, Joaquim stood with Aaron by the communal olive press and nodded toward the next man in line. The villager stepped forward and poured his basketful into the shallow stone tray, and Aaron spread the newly harvested olives into a single layer.

Joaquim checked the donkey's harness to be sure it hadn't slipped from the axle on the grinding stone. He was about to pull the animal forward on the circular track when Aaron reached out and stopped him. "Listen," he said, a thread of warning in his voice. "Horses."

Joaquim stood still and heard the sound of drumming hooves. Since no one in Nazareth owned a horse, this could not be good news. Joaquim jerked his chin toward the waiting man, then gestured to the clearing in the center of the marketplace. "Let us wait a moment, my friend."

They did not have to wait long. A quartet of horses trotted into town, scattering several villagers and drawing others from their homes and market booths. The riders pulled up in a clearing. A guard in heavy armor dismounted and tossed the reins to a villager who waited in silence. "Water the animals," he said, scarcely looking at the man to whom he spoke. "Be quick about it."

Joaquim folded his arms and looked around the rapidly growing crowd. His Anna and another woman stood behind the horses, as skittish as the beasts. Joseph had emerged from his house to check out the trouble, and in a narrow lane Joaquim recognized his daughter's veiled head. Like a wise woman, however, Mary remained in the shadows at the edge of the crowd.

Joaquim's stomach tightened when the second rider dismounted. He knew this pale-skinned man—the fellow was the tax collector who had demanded Joaquim's mule. What had he come to steal this time?

"Townspeople of Nazareth," the foreigner called, his voice echoing above the squeaking of his companions' saddles, "in the name of your king, Herod, and the almighty Caesar Augustus, you are hereby ordered to participate in a census."

A buzzing of voices, a palpable unease, rolled through the crowd and retreated only when the blue-eyed foreigner lifted his hand. "Every man will return to the land of his ancestors, along with each member of his family, there to be counted."

The buzzing grew more pronounced, and this time Joaquim could hear grumbled protests.

Joseph was the first to find his courage. He stepped forward and gestured for the tax collector's attention. "And what if that land is a hundred miles away?"

The tax gatherer smiled in sudden silence. "Then you would be wise to leave as soon as possible." His expression hardened as he focused his frosty attention on Joseph. "You have one month to comply with the order. Any resistance will be firmly answered . . . with force, if necessary." The tax collector turned his back to the crowd—a risky move, even with armed guards to protect him—and mounted his horse.

The burly soldier on the ground placed his hand on his sword, silently daring any protestor to argue the point; then he, too, mounted and spurred his beast.

Herod's men departed as abruptly as they had arrived.

Aaron turned to Joaquim, his face flaming. "This is how it will be with this king and the king after that. We will never have peace, not as long as we live under the shadow of foreign rulers."

Joaquim drew a breath to answer, then saw his son-in-law shouldering his way through the crowd. He swallowed his words and forced his face into neutral, pleasant lines. Joseph had borne enough grief; he did not need yet another burden on his shoulders.

✣

Mary felt the protective pressure of Joseph's eyes on her as her family welcomed the young couple to their evening meal. Her father sat on his mat at the head of the circle with Aaron on one side and Joseph on the other. Hannah and Hodiya squeezed between their father and Grandfather Avram.

Mary and her mother did not sit but worked during the meal, keeping the stewpot stirred, the bread basket filled, and the fruit bowl replenished.

Her father took a handful of olives, then tossed one in his mouth. "A census can mean only one thing." He looked at Grandfather Avram. "More taxes. For Herod. For Rome."

Hannah reached for a piece of bread, but Hodiya's arms were longer. The two girls began to squabble, and Mary silenced them with a stern look.

"Rome will always want our lifeblood," her grandfather responded, his voice creaking. "Caesar keeps us humble by keeping us poor."

"No good will come out of this census," Aaron insisted. "Who will tend to our work while we stand in line? Who will pay the wages of those who are hired to record our names? We will, through our taxes."

Her father dipped his bread into a bowl of olive oil and herbs. "Isra'el learned a painful lesson when David was punished for taking a census. If we must be counted, let ADONAI do the counting."

Aaron snorted. "At least we are able to register here. I hear the rabbi has to travel all the way to Capernaum. The journey will take him at least two days."

"Two days away from his work." Mary's father shook his head. "A shame."

Mary's stomach tightened when Joseph lowered his bread. "I cannot register in Nazareth."

Silence, as thick as wool, wrapped around the gathering as the other men stared at her husband.

"The order," Joseph continued, "was for each man to return to the place of his ancestors. So I must travel to Bethlehem."

Mary's mother shot her a worried glance, then knelt at Joseph's side. "Surely not! The journey to Bethlehem is more than a hundred miles. It would not be good for you to be away so long."

"I won't be traveling alone. Each member of my family must go as well."

"Of course your father and brother will go," Aaron said, shrugging. "They are certainly of age."

Joseph raised his eyes to Mary's face in an oddly keen look. "I wasn't speaking of my father or brother."

Mary followed her mother's example and knelt as realization bloomed in her chest.

"My father and brother have to finish a boat they're building at the shore," Joseph said. "They will make the journey later, when they've finished. I want to leave tomorrow . . . because waiting will not benefit my wife."

Mary blinked as his words took hold in her thoughts. Bethlehem? The birthplace of King David was as distant as Juttah; the journey would take at least a week. Then they would have to register, and after that they would have to return—

"No." Her mother's voice cut the silence. "Mary must stay here. No one can expect a woman in her condition—"

"The Romans do not make exceptions." Joaquim caught Joseph's eye. "You are right. Mary must go and we must accept it."

Mary struggled for words to make the inescapable easier to bear. "Mother, the journey is not so long. I may be able to go and return before—"

Her mother's nostrils flared. "That is for ADONAI to decide, not you."

Mary almost laughed. *Now* her mother was willing for ADONAI's will to be done? Yet apparently the Lord had decided she should take this trip.

She straightened her spine and moved her gaze to Joseph's. Those deep brown wells, which she used to find inscrutable, now supplied her with strength. "I am going," she said simply, "with my husband."

Her mother gasped, her hand flying to her mouth, but when Mary looked at her father, something like grudging admiration had filled his eyes. He glanced at the bulge of her belly; then he spoke to Joseph in the no-nonsense tone one man uses with another. "You should leave in the morning. Do not waste time on the road."

"I will protect her," Joseph said. "And the child."

"The road around Samaria is the safest"—Joaquim continued as if he hadn't heard—"but the straight road is the most direct. Go through Samaria if the way feels right to you, but do not linger there."

At the mention of Samaria, a dart of fear entered Mary's heart. Relations between the Jews and the Samaritans had never been good, but last month her village learned of a group from Nain who'd been beaten and robbed along a Samaritan highway. So many stories of murdered Jerusalem pilgrims abounded that few people dared to take the most direct route south.

Joseph lifted his chin and boldly met her father's eyes. "I promise you. I will protect Mary and the child with my life."

Dawn came reluctantly the next morning, the sun peering through clouds heavy with the promise of rain. Mary stood in her parents' courtyard next to Joseph's donkey, her hands resting upon her swollen stomach, her heart about to burst with concerns and fears she dared not speak.

Her father had offered the use of his mule, but Joseph refused to inconvenience her family. Her husband had been willing, however, to accept two waterskins, a bag of grain for the donkey, and several bundles of bread, cheese, and fruit. These he had tied together and slung over the haircloth saddle, along with a pair of blankets, in case they needed to sleep by the side of the road.

"The first well is five miles south," Mary's mother said, pressing three coins into her daughter's palm. "Make sure you reserve plenty of food if you travel through Samaria. People may not want to sell to you there, but if they do—"

"I cannot take your last shekels." Mary tried to push the money back into her mother's hand. "ADONAI will provide for us."

Her mother closed Mary's fingers around the coins and looked at her with eyes that had gone soft with gentleness. "Perhaps he just has."

Overwhelmed by a rush of gratitude, Mary embraced her mother. "Take care of Father and the girls."

"And you . . . take care of yourself and that baby. And Joseph, too, of course." Her mother stepped back and gazed at her with a watery smile. "I pray you are hearing ADONAI's will more clearly than I."

Mary's father tested the bindings on the donkey's harness. "Fine," he said, gruffly approving Joseph's preparation. He hauled his gaze from the donkey and focused on his daughter. "Mary," he said, his voice growing thick, "you are a strong young woman."

"Perhaps I have you to thank for that." Mary embraced him, then said quick farewells to her grandfather, uncle, and cousins.

Finally, she turned to Joseph. "I am ready, Husband."

They walked several miles, making their way toward the great road that led south through Samaria. Mary noted Joseph's choice and bit her lip, torn between urging him to take the longer, safer route and resting in the knowledge that he was taking the shorter road to spare her discomfort.

Finally, she decided to hold her tongue. If her husband could trust ADONAI to see them safely through the hostile region, so could she.

Like a respectful wife, Mary walked behind her husband as he led their pack animal. Though she set out with a determined heart and an energetic step, the extra weight she carried soon sapped her strength. Joseph must have intuited her failing spirits or heard her flagging steps, but whenever he turned to check on her, she lifted her chin and gave him a confident smile, determined not to slow his pace.

By midday, however, as she struggled to maintain her balance on the steeply descending road, she could not summon the strength to feign confidence. At one point a Roman chariot thundered toward them, and Joseph pulled the donkey off the highway as required by law. Mary stepped off the pavement and felt her knees give way in the soft soil. Unable even to lift her head, she allowed herself to crumple on the earth and closed her eyes, content to let the world gallop by.

Within a moment, Joseph knelt at her side. "Mary! Are you all right?"

She nodded drowsily and kept her eyes closed. "Just let me rest . . . until the chariot passes."

She heard Joseph catch his breath, then the crunch of his sandals on the gravel as he moved to the edge of the road. The chariot roared past in a tumult of hooves and shouts.

Joseph's strong hands supported her arm and neck. "You are going to ride," he said, his voice as firm as her father's had ever been. "The donkey can carry you."

Her eyes flew open. "The donkey has to carry our supplies."

"*I'll* carry the supplies."

She stared at him in amused wonder. "Joseph, you will be the laughingstock of Galilee. No man puts his pack on his back and his wife on his beast. Let me walk behind you; it's my place."

"Mary." Determination had dilated his pupils, turning his eyes into fathomless black pools. "You are my wife; it's your place to obey. And I say you will ride the donkey."

Mary drew a breath to protest again, then snapped her mouth shut. The man had already sullied his reputation to salvage hers. After marrying her in a visible state of pregnancy, why should he care if a few strangers thought him odd?

She slipped her arm over his shoulder and let herself be helped up. "The donkey," she said, her hands resting atop her belly as Joseph unloaded the animal, "he won't know what to do with me."

"He won't need to know." Joseph grinned at her. "I'll lead him every step of the way."

※

For two days Mary and Joseph traveled over the wide Roman road that led through the mountainous border of lower Galilee and opened into the wide Plain of Esdraelon. They watered the animal whenever they happened upon a creek or a brook; they refilled their waterskins and nibbled on bread, dried figs, and cheese. The broad plain faded behind them as they approached Samaria, where few children of Isra'el dared to travel.

Though Mary had been perspiring all day, she went slick with the sour sweat of anxiety when they neared the village of Ginaea. Uniformed sentries guarded the road near the village gates, and they were stopping every traveler.

She noted the straight line of Joseph's shoulders and the forward jut of his jaw. He had seen the sentries too, probably long before she did.

"Will we have trouble?"

Joseph did not answer but gave her a thin smile.

As they fell in line with the other travelers, Mary caught several people staring at her and her husband. Of all the wayfarers on the road—men, women, and children leading donkeys, camels, and mules—she was the only woman riding a beast.

She started to slip down and walk behind Joseph, but he reached out and caught her sleeve. "Stay put."

"But—"

"Remain on the animal. I don't want you within arm's reach of these men."

At last they reached the checkpoint. This close, she could see that though the two guards wore the iron-and-leather armor of Roman soldiers, their pale features and red hair indicated their status as Herod's mercenaries.

The first bored-looking guard studied Joseph's face. "Where are you headed on the king's road?"

"From Nazareth," Joseph answered. "To Bethlehem. For the census."

The guard snorted. "From cesspool to cesspool."

The second soldier looked at Mary, the corner of his mouth twitching. "Your woman rides?"

"My *wife*," Joseph stressed, "is with child."

Increasingly uncomfortable beneath the soldier's icy gaze, Mary lowered her head.

"This," the second guard said to his companion, "is no leader of men. Move them along."

Mary exhaled in quiet relief when Joseph pulled the donkey toward the village. Among so many people, maybe she wouldn't feel quite so conspicuous.

Indeed, Ginaea was a bright contrast to the stark countryside through which they'd been traveling. The crowded market teemed with farmers, fishermen, and glassmakers, whose goods sold alongside those of workers with brass and iron. Women sold silks and woolens in canopied booths, while an Essene, recognizable by his spotless white tunic, walked through the crowd quoting the words of the prophets: "'Rejoice greatly, O daughter of Zion! Shout in triumph, O people of Jerusalem! Look, your king is coming to you. He is righteous and victorious, yet he is humble, riding on a donkey—'"

The Essene halted when his gaze crossed Mary's.

His startled look so embarrassed her that she looked away. As heat crept into her face, she reached for Joseph's hand and squeezed it. When he stopped, a question in his eyes, she slipped from the saddle. "It will feel good to walk a bit," she said, resting one hand on top of her belly.

He did not argue but led her through the crowded marketplace. A young girl wandered up and flashed a dimple at Mary, then took her hand as if she would ask her to dance.

Mary laughed. "My dancing days are behind me, little one."

The grinning girl twirled under Mary's arm, then broke her hold and pointed to a booth stocked with colored threads, yarns, and ribbons.

"So lovely," Mary whispered. She tugged on Joseph's sleeve to let him know where she was going and stepped closer to the booth. The little girl's mother pulled out a length of red silk ribbon. "I'm sorry." Mary spread her empty hands. "I cannot buy."

The woman's eyes softened. She pulled a length of red ribbon from a spool and placed it across Mary's palm. "A gift," she said simply, a dimple showing in her own cheek. "For your child."

A blush warmed Mary's face at the unexpected gesture. "Thank you."

The woman dropped her hands to her little girl's shoulders, then gave Mary a mother-to-mother smile. "The baby will come soon," she said, appraising Mary's belly. "You carry him like a son."

Mary wrapped her fingers around the ribbon as Joseph stepped to her side.

"To see yourself in a young one," the woman continued, looking now at Joseph, "there is no greater joy."

Mary tore her gaze from the obvious mother and daughter to look up at Joseph. She feared she would see embarrassment or denial in his face, but his smile retained its usual expression of good humor.

She thanked the woman again and clung to Joseph's sleeve as he led her back toward the donkey.

The crowd grew quieter and less boisterous as they neared the synagogue. Mary walked only a step behind Joseph as the Essene came walking toward them from another alley, his rumbling words preceding him like a trumpet call: "'. . . and his dominion will be from sea to sea and from the river to the ends of the earth. . . .'"

Joseph halted so suddenly that Mary stumbled into his back. Alarmed, she peeked around her husband's shoulder and saw one of Herod's mounted guards beside the synagogue. The soldier watched the bold Essene with narrowed eyes, one hand on the hilt of his sword.

Too late, the Essene turned, saw the soldier, and slowly lifted his gaze. He fell silent and turned toward another alley, only to find it blocked by another guard on horseback.

Both soldiers watched the Essene, their features hardening in menacing stares of disapproval.

The trapped man lifted his eyes to heaven as if appealing to a higher authority, then looked at Mary. "Thus," said the man, raising a trembling hand, "says ADONAI my God, who has promised to send our Messiah."

A sudden chill climbed the ladder of Mary's spine as the Essene bowed his head. The first soldier drew his sword and spurred his horse forward, but Joseph whirled Mary around, shielding her from the horrible and bloody sight.

chapter twenty-two

As relaxed as a fat cat, Melchior sat astride his camel, his head dipping in time to the camel's plodding gait. A dusty Mesopotamian village lay on the horizon, and even from this vantage point he could tell that prosperity, if it had ever visited the place, had left few traces of its presence.

From various portals in cinnamon-colored mud huts, dozens of scrawny children emerged like hungry rats, drawn by the sight of the approaching caravan.

Melchior glanced behind him to see if either Gaspar or Balthasar might want to stop, but neither showed any inclination to visit such a godforsaken village. The market situated outside the gates featured a pair of stalls; these held a few baskets filled with shriveled roots and dried produce.

Gaspar trotted up beside Melchior, a luscious cluster of dates in his hand. "A good thing I brought the extra pack camel, no?"

Balthasar, riding on Melchior's left, considered the pitiful market with disdain, then folded his arms atop his saddle. "Perhaps we should have brought another. We could have spared something to feed these pitiful urchins."

Melchior heaved a sigh and shook his head at a persistent lad who ran alongside his camel with a half-dead kitten in his grip.

"Shoo, go on," he said, flapping his hand at the boy. "I have no use for such things. . . . Tell me, Gaspar," he called, fishing in his money belt for a copper coin, "how many days has it been since we departed?"

Gaspar stared down his nose at the boy who caught and kissed the copper coin Melchior threw. "One hundred and four."

"And how many of those days have you spoken with regret of your decision to journey with us?"

The line of Balthasar's mouth curved in his bearded face. "One hundred and five." He leaned forward in the saddle. "I am already counting tomorrow."

Gaspar harrumphed and urged his mount forward, resentment evident in the slight curl of his upper lip.

They traveled for a while in silence; then Gaspar slowed until they were once again riding abreast.

Melchior smiled, pleased to see this sign of softening in his former pupil. Gaspar was a brilliant thinker, but he was young and still far too distracted by the pleasures of the world.

"Tell me, Gaspar," Melchior said, crossing his hands at the wrist as he leaned forward, "do the words of the prophets arouse none of your curiosity? The star we follow bespeaks a king. His mother. His father. And still you talk of the ancient prophecies as if they were nothing more than the foolish musings of a madman."

"*Several* madmen," Balthasar interjected. "Several prophets, including our own rab-mag, wrote in different countries and at different times, yet they all spoke of an anointed king who will come from Israel."

Gaspar twisted in the saddle to face his tormentors. "You have shown me stars. You have told me stories. But none of your evidence is conclusive. You say there is one true and invisible God, but I have never heard him. He may have spoken to Belteshazzar, but he has never spoken to me."

Melchior straightened and picked up his reins. "I have seen more than enough evidence to bolster my faith. So the lack, therefore, must lie in you, Gaspar, and not in the true God." He smiled and kicked his camel, urging the gangly beast into a trot.

The star had appeared in the blue sky of the west, bright enough to pierce the fading light of a hot afternoon . . . but not bright enough to dispel Gaspar's doubt.

chapter twenty-three

After safely traversing Samaria, one day slid almost seamlessly into the next. Mary and Joseph traveled, they stopped, they ate, and they watered the donkey. Whenever the sun neared the western horizon, they looked for a village where they could pass the night with other children of Isra'el who exercised the law of hospitality.

The unusual events that shaped their lives had wrought a certain formality between them that continued even after their wedding. Yet, perched atop the donkey like some prized and rare treasure, Mary discovered the unusual delight of conversing with her husband. Few wives in Nazareth, she realized, ever experienced the luxury of having nothing to do but sit and talk to the men who had promised to stand by them for a lifetime.

One afternoon she cast Joseph a shy glance and brought up a subject he had never broached. "You never told me, Husband, of your dream."

He smiled at the ground. "I dream every night."

"I'm sure you do . . . but not of holy things."

He studied her, a look of inward intentness taking shape in his eyes. "What if I can't remember?"

"Please." She reached out and touched his hand, tight around the donkey's reins. "Will you tell me?"

Joseph lifted his head and scanned the horizon. "I saw a man," he finally said, "but not an ordinary man. He told me the child within you had been conceived by the Ruach HaKodesh. And I should not be afraid."

Mary waited, assuming that Joseph was sorting through his memories, but he said no more. "Is that all you saw?"

"I told you . . . I dream every night."

So he had seen more . . . and he would not share the rest of it with her. She lowered her head to look up into his face. "*Are* you afraid?"

He barked a laugh. "Not anymore." His gaze remained on the road, as if he could not look at her and risk revealing his true feelings. But she heard a tremor of uncertainty in his voice when he asked, "Are you?"

"Not at all."

He looked at her, surprise in his eyes, and laughed when he saw her deliberately blank face. They were lying, both of them, for how could they help being terrified by the responsibility of ushering the hope of the world into a hopeless place?

They continued, the silence broken only by the clip-clop of the donkey's hooves. Then Mary asked the question that had been haunting her for weeks. "How do we raise such a child?"

The donkey snorted and shook his head, jangling the bit in his mouth. When the animal had settled, Joseph glanced at her. "With an eye toward God. So we can keep him from harm."

"And if we can't? How do we answer to God for our failure?"

Her questions fell, like the cry of the raven circling overhead, unanswered.

chapter twenty-four

Herod's youngest son, Antipas, a copy of his royal father in all but girth, knelt before the throne and kissed the king's age-spotted hand. Herod studied his son, weighed the motivation behind the kiss and the act of homage, and decided to let this son live another day.

Antipas lifted his head and dared meet the royal gaze. "The king requests my presence?"

Herod dismissed the guards hovering near the entrance to the throne room with a flick of the wrist. "Leave us."

When the two men were alone, Herod looked his son in the eye. "This census. It has revealed an opposition to my rule that concerns me."

Still on one knee, Antipas winced in exaggerated remorse. "Surely not."

"Do you doubt my word?"

The son bowed his head. "Never, Father. But men may say all sorts of things when they are in their cups or on a journey and bragging around a campfire."

"This opposition may advance beyond mere words."

Antipas frowned, then blinked as Herod's meaning took hold. "The kingdom will be yours, Father, until the last of your breaths."

Herod rose from his throne. "*You* are the opposition I speak of, Antipas! I hear rumors that my subjects will rise against me, and what do I hear from my own son? I hear arguments! I hear silence!"

Antipas blanched and pushed himself up from the floor.

"Judea," Herod continued, pacing before the chamber's most elaborately painted wall. "Samaria. Galilee. All of them talk of this prophetic king, this man who will defeat me, and yet you do not speak against it?"

"Father, Excellency—" Antipas stumbled over his words—"you have no greater ally than the man who stands before you now."

Herod turned and placed his hand on the fleshy cheek of his son. A weakling, this one. He would never hold the entire kingdom. "I know of your loyalty." Herod adopted a soothing tone. "I do. Because we are the same, you and me. And the man who inherits my kingdom must have the same intentions—the same resolve—that I do."

He patted Antipas's flaccid cheek, then turned and braced his hands on the back of a gilded chair. "Hear me when I tell you this, my son. You will not live to sit upon my throne if you fail me now." He kept his eyes on the chair in his grasp, but heard Antipas's quickened breathing.

"What—what would you have me do, Father?"

"I had a wife betray me," Herod continued, ignoring the question. "I had two sons do the same. Where are they now?"

"Th-they are," Antipas stuttered, "no more."

Herod lifted his hand and slapped it back to the chair. "I will have this threat to my kingdom removed as well. I will end this threat as I end all threats. And you, my son, must help me."

Antipas fell to his knee again, not in homage this time but in dread. "Command me, Father."

"I will," Herod answered. "In time."

Because of the jostling crowds on the Roman highway—and, Mary suspected, the frequent snide comments they overheard from travelers of all nationalities—Joseph left the wide paved road and followed a well-worn footpath that would lead them through the mountainous wilderness of Judea.

She said nothing when he chose to leave the road and fully expected him to justify his action with some excuse. She wasn't prepared for brutal honesty.

"I was tired," he said, well after they had left the highway, "of men looking at you like that."

A flurry of emotions ruffled through her—pleasure at his protectiveness, confusion as to his exact meaning, irritation that he might have jeopardized their safety because of some assault to his male pride—so she answered him with an honest response of her own. "How, exactly—" she peered at him over the edge of her veil—"were they looking at me?"

Joseph tilted his sunburned face up at her, a smile crinkling the corners of his eyes. "Like you were one of those spoiled Roman women who ride around in litters. As if you weren't willing to get a little dust between your toes."

The idea that anyone might think her spoiled brought laughter floating up from Mary's throat. She laughed until the baby kicked her ribs; then she released a last crowing whoop and covered the remainder of her giggles with coughing.

Finally, she caught her breath. "Joseph ben Jacob," she said, smiling fondly at the back of her husband's head, "you have a most vibrant imagination."

The pleasure of that exchange warmed her until Joseph pulled the donkey aside at a small creek. Mary dismounted and walked to stretch her legs while Joseph watered the animal.

She paused, the wind blowing her veil, as another traveling party came into view: a man, a woman, a donkey. Though the pack animal did not carry much, it seemed to stagger under its load.

Mary waved at the woman as they passed.

"They did not stop," she murmured when the strangers continued on their way.

"Their animal is starving," Joseph answered, gripping the neck of their own donkey. "I could count his ribs from where I stood."

He turned, offering his hand to Mary.

She glanced at their own thin beast and shook her head. "I think I would like to walk awhile," she said, shading her eyes with her hand. "I hear a little walking is good for the baby."

The evening shadows had begun to stretch across the rocky hills by the time Joseph found a suitable place of shelter. He helped Mary from the donkey before he led the animal to water.

From a sheltered spot behind a ledge, Mary watched her husband care for the animal. He made certain the beast could drink and rest before applying the hobbles to his hind legs; then he patted the donkey's neck and approached the rise where she waited.

She pulled bread, cheese, and dried figs from the leather satchel and spread the food on a cloth. Joseph sat across from her and offered the prayer of blessing, then sipped from the waterskin while she nibbled at her bread.

Her husband, she couldn't help but notice, did not eat.

She frowned. "You must be hungry. You must eat something to keep up your strength."

"I will. When you are settled."

She finished quickly, conscious of his protective gaze, smoothed the blanket, and slowly stretched out on her side. Her eyes burned from weariness, and her bones felt as though they'd been rattled like seeds in a dry gourd. She exhaled a long sigh and closed her eyes, ready for sleep.

But sleep did not come, not right away. She heard Joseph moving and lifted one eyelid in time to see him scoop his portion of the dried figs into his palm. He left the bread and cheese on the blanket where he would sleep but carried the figs down the hill.

Mary's exhaustion faded as curiosity sparked her blood. She pushed herself up and peered over the edge of the rocks at the scene below. The western sky still glowed with remnants of twilight, and a bright star shone above the horizon, tinting the scene with silver.

She caught her breath as Joseph ambled toward the donkey. The startled animal jerked and brayed as Joseph's step crunched the gravel;

then he caught the scent of food. Donkey lips peeled back and yellowed teeth grabbed a fig with almost dainty precision.

Joseph stood in the silver light, rubbing the animal's neck as the beast ate a good portion of his master's dinner. "That's it," he said, slapping the animal's haunches. The donkey nibbled at his sleeve as if asking for more, and Joseph chuckled. "I am the hungry one. Not you."

As Joseph climbed back up to their shelter, Mary crept to her blanket. She draped one hand across her face, drawing the deep breaths of exhausted sleep while watching the man who was her husband.

Joseph ate his bread and cheese; he drank a long draught from the waterskin. Then he lay down upon the narrow slip of wool, pillowing his head with his hands as he stared at the night sky.

Just before he closed his eyes, she heard him murmur a prayer: "If I am doing your will, ADONAI . . . as you would have me do it, I pray you would give me a sign."

Mary waited, half expecting Gabriel to appear and affirm Joseph's actions, but the only answer that came to her ears was the deep and steady sound of her husband's snoring.

chapter twenty-five

The next day their footpath merged again with the southern highway. Mary walked for a while, but when the baby grew restless, she gratefully obeyed Joseph's urging to ride. The donkey seemed in fine fettle this morning, especially since he'd enjoyed a good breakfast of desert grass while they waited to pass through a sentry point.

Now the traffic slowed again, but she could see no sign of soldiers or horses on the road ahead. "What seems to be the problem?" she asked.

"A river." Joseph pointed. "There's a ford up ahead, so we must all cross there. The water is too fast and deep everywhere else."

Mary fell silent. The Jordan was the largest river in the region, but occasionally rainfall swept over the mountains and entered wadis that had been cut years before. These wadis formed short-lived, often violent streams, creating havoc for travelers who had to cross or go miles out of their way.

She waited with the others until they reached the edge of the muddy brown water. The current moved swiftly, but the other side lay only a short distance away. The bottleneck had resulted because this bank had the most gradual approach to the water's edge.

"Hold tight to the donkey's mane," Joseph told her, leading the animal into the fast-moving stream. "We'll be through before you can name the twelve sons of Jacob."

Mary stared at the swirling current as a sense of unease crept into her mood. "Reuben," she began, twisting her fingers in the animal's hair as Joseph led them forward. "Simeon and Levi. Judah, Zebulun, and Issachar."

She caught her breath when the water crept to Joseph's waist. The donkey's ears went flat against his skull as he brayed in protest. "I don't blame you," she whispered, leaning forward. "I wouldn't want to walk through this either, but I know you can trust the one who leads you."

Joseph moved farther, his staff in one hand and the donkey's reins in the other. Mary winced when she realized that water had covered many of the goods strapped to her husband's back. Tonight they would drink from mud-covered waterskins and eat muddy cheese. But at least they had cheese to eat.

"Dan and Gad," she said, remembering her list. "Asher and Naphtali."

She gasped as the donkey's feet slipped from beneath him. Water rushed up to cover her thighs. She realized the animal was *swimming*.

"Joseph," she recited, "and Benjamin. Twelve sons of Jacob, born to him from Rachel and Leah—"

Her voice caught in her throat as an odd ripple shimmied across the water. Something was swimming behind Joseph, a living thing moving toward her and the donkey.

The donkey must have recognized the water snake just as she did, for he brayed and tossed his head, jerking the slippery reins from Joseph's grasp. Mary lost her grip on the panicked animal and spilled headlong into the stream, screaming as the current pressed her head beneath the surface. She opened her eyes, saw nothing but darkness, and felt the world shift as up and down and right and left tumbled about in confusion.

She clawed through liquid mud, opened her mouth, and tasted terror. She fought against waters that carried her far from Joseph and safety and the role she had been chosen to fulfill. She struggled to lift her head, to find some purchase with her feet or hands, but nothing would support her weight.

She had just closed her eyes in resignation when a strong hand

encircled the back of her neck. As someone pulled her from the tena-
cious water, she heard the thwack of the river's broken hold. Suddenly
she was coughing and weeping, trembling in Joseph's arms.

His face, as wet and muddy as her own, loomed only inches from
hers. "Mary," he whispered, and in his eyes she saw not the respect a
righteous man feels for his mission but the love a man feels for his wife.
"I would not lose you now!"

Coughing, laughing, she let her head fall to his shoulder and shivered in the warmth of his embrace. "Joseph." Her wet hand rose to
touch his face. "I will not be easily lost."

That night, as they dried their wet garments and sandals by a crackling
fire, Mary's gaze drifted to her husband's tanned legs. He had walked
for days, and his feet were bleeding. His sandals, wet from the river, had
chafed against callused skin and formed blisters. Those had burst, and
now blood stained the sand where he sat.

"Joseph." A note of reproach lined her voice.

"What?" He looked at her, honest surprise on his face, and did not
realize her intent until she wet her veil in fresh water and knelt before
him. "No," he said, catching her wrists. "The mother of my Lord is not
to wash my feet."

She broke his hold, then spoke with quiet firmness. "Your wife is
happy to serve you . . . as you have served her these many days."

He made a sound deep in his throat, but he did not protest again
as she washed the sand out of the open wounds.

As she worked, she whispered to the baby who slept beneath her
ribs. "You will have a good and decent man to raise you. A man who
will give all he has . . . out of love."

chapter twenty-six

Mary knew they were nearing the Holy City when they were yet a half-day's journey from Jerusalem. The highway became more crowded, their fellow travelers more animated and joyful. Though it was not festival season, when the city's population would swell by thousands, tradition, teaching, and ADONAI himself had burned a love for Jerusalem into every Hebrew heart.

Rocked by the donkey's gait, she closed her eyes and dropped down the well of memory to the afternoon she and her parents had last visited the Holy City. Her father had joined others in singing one of the psalms reserved for the ascent to Jerusalem . . . even as people were singing it now.

She opened her eyes and smiled as she listened to voices on the wind:

> For ADONAI has chosen Jerusalem;
> he has desired it as his home.
> "This is my home where I will live forever," he said.
> "I will live here, for this is the place I desired.
> I will make this city prosperous
> and satisfy its poor with food.
> I will make its priests the agents of salvation;
> its godly people will sing for joy.

Here I will increase the power of David;
my anointed one will be a light for my people.
I will clothe his enemies with shame,
but he will be a glorious king."

Mary looked at Joseph, awareness thickening between them, as the pilgrims on the road sang of the Anointed One. The Messiah— the baby she carried—would be a light for these people, a glorious king.

Her weariness lifted when the gleaming city came into view. Not even the sight of Roman soldiers at the gates could dispel her joy, for she carried the hope of her people within her.

"I don't understand," she whispered when Joseph looked at her, "but I feel it. Don't you?"

He nodded, his eyes shiny with hope.

As they neared the gate, Mary slipped from the donkey and walked behind her husband, remaining close to Joseph as they entered the tumult and cacophony that defined Jerusalem.

They passed the markets, where round-eyed foreigners spoke in strange tongues and offered delicacies for sale. Merchants from Mary's region bargained with buyers from Italy, Greece, and Egypt in the broad accents of Galileans. Laughing Gentiles fingered silks and linens, metals and glass, while the aromas of cooked meats combined with the pungent odors of cattle and goats. White-robed priests threaded their way through the crowd, frowning at curled and bejeweled foreign women who rode in slave-carried, curtained litters. Pharisees stood on balconies, their broad phylacteries and wide fringes swaying in the breeze, while mounted soldiers picked their way through the throngs in the street.

Mary's stomach tightened as they passed a booth where a young woman offered fried locusts and fruitcake along with oil and wine. For nearly a week she had eaten nothing but bread, cheese, and dried fruit, yet she would not be likely to taste anything else until they reached their destination.

"Hello?" A woman in bright jewelry and sheer veils called to them, her smile a shade more brazen than was modest. "Would you like to buy some jewelry for your beautiful wife?"

Joseph, Mary noticed, did not let his eyes linger on the bejeweled woman.

She startled when a man hissed at her from the crowd. "The donkey." The stranger jerked his head toward their animal. "He is a strong beast. Would your husband be willing to sell him?"

Mary glanced at Joseph, who had stopped due to the heavy pedestrian traffic. "You should speak to him."

The stranger moved closer, one hand stroking the donkey's clipped mane. "Such a fine animal."

Mary was about to tug on Joseph's robe when her husband turned, one hand shooting toward the stranger. She gasped when Joseph's wrist closed around the man's free hand, which had gripped the strap of the satchel hanging from the donkey's saddle.

"What's ours," Joseph said, his voice like flint, "is ours."

The stranger offered Joseph a sly half smile and slunk away, blending into the crowd.

Mary looked at the satchel, knowing that it contained their only shekels and the last of their food. If Joseph had been even a little less observant . . .

She exhaled in relief when he led her down a quieter alley. Several merchant shops lined this narrow road, and among the crowd she spotted several white-robed priests.

One of them stood on a corner, calling to anyone who would listen. " 'See, my servant will prosper; he will be highly exalted,' " he shouted, his skin parched and lined from exposure to the sun. "'Many were amazed when they saw him—beaten and bloodied, so disfigured one would scarcely know he was a person. And he will again startle many nations. Kings will stand speechless in his presence. For they will see what they had not previously been told about; they will understand what they had not heard about.'"

His roving gaze fastened upon Mary. "And a sword," he said, unsmiling, "will pierce your soul."

She shifted her eyes to the safety of Joseph's broad shoulders, but something in the priest's unflinching stare unsettled her. She glanced back to see if he was repeating the phrase to other passersby, but when she turned, he had gone.

Mary sighed when they exited the southwestern gate of Jerusalem, but a forlorn sight outside the city walls chilled her blood. On a bald knoll near the valley used to burn refuse, a company of Roman soldiers was overseeing the crucifixion of two criminals, a harsh form of execution she had heard about but had never witnessed.

Overwhelmed by the pitiful cries of the condemned, she cried out and buried her face in Joseph's shoulder.

"I know," Joseph said, his eyes darkening. "Leave it to the Romans to devise such a cruel punishment."

Mary lifted her head. She should be stronger; she didn't want Joseph to think her weak. But some of the things she'd seen on this journey had made her wonder if her father was right—why would ADONAI send the Messiah at a time when all the world seemed set against Isra'el? She had never seen such evil, and the hope she carried was a vulnerable child. . . .

"Things will be quieter now," Joseph said, his tone gentle and undoubtedly meant to reassure her. "Bethlehem is a small town, nothing like Jerusalem."

Mary looked down the road and saw trees, fields, and a few grazing sheep. Perhaps, finally, they were nearing the end of their journey.

Joseph helped her mount the donkey and launched into a psalm of David that lifted her spirits. He fell silent, however, as they overtook a young man who ambled by the side of the road, a shepherd's staff in one hand and a flock trailing behind him.

When they passed the man, Mary turned to examine him. Though the shepherd could not have seen more than twenty summers, his face was as weather-beaten and scored as the rocks on the road. He acknowledged her with the barest of nods, then turned his eyes toward the walled village in the distance.

Joseph spoke in a low voice. "Those sheep are destined for sacrifice in the Temple. The men who keep them are outcasts, because shepherds cannot observe the Sabbath or keep the Law."

"Then why do they become shepherds?"

"They are broken men, Mary. Some of them have been cast out because of their dealings with the Romans; others are sick or were unclean before they began to keep the beasts. They have no other place to go."

Joseph did not have to say more. Mary had seen outcasts gleaning in the fields outside Nazareth—women with strange bleeding illnesses and men who had contracted leprosy. Unable to meet the strict standards of the Law, they were forced to move to Gentile villages or live outside society.

Her throat ached with regret. ADONAI had exalted a poor girl and called a common carpenter. Clearly he had chosen to use the most humble of his servants, so did he have a plan for men like this dispirited shepherd?

Within the private curtain of her mantle, she pressed her hands to the round warmth of her belly. At least Joseph would teach her baby a trade. If ADONAI willed, her son would never have to spend lonely days and nights wandering in search of lost sheep.

chapter twenty-seven

Melchior groaned in relief as the caravan entered the chiseled walls of Jerusalem. The camel's jolting gait had reduced his muscles to mush, and the wrinkles on his face had filled with grit.

He glanced behind him, where Gaspar was happily playing the part of visiting sultan and waving to those who cast curious glances in their direction.

"Gaspar!" Melchior said, his voice hoarse with frustration. "Have you forgotten our purpose for this journey?"

"How could I?" Gaspar bent to wave at a particularly pretty Roman woman who peeked up at him from between the curtains of her litter. "It is all you have talked about for months."

The camels moved slowly, regally, through the crowd and stopped when a group of uniformed Roman soldiers blocked the street.

"Halt!" one of the men called. As he stepped forward, Melchior recognized the red plume on his helmet.

"Good day to you, Centurion." Melchior spoke in Greek, the lingua franca of the region. He pulled a gold coin from the pouch at his side and held it up, making sure it caught the sun.

The centurion recognized the flash of gold. "Good day to you. Where might you and your companions be going?"

Melchior dropped the coin and was not at all surprised to see it land safely in the soldier's palm. "Oh, dear. How clumsy of me."

The centurion brushed the coin on the sleeve of his short tunic and grinned. "May I help you find your way through Jerusalem? Provide a safe escort, perhaps?"

"I am sure you may. My companions and I are searching for a king—one that has been mentioned many times in the Hebrew prophecies. In the East, we saw his star . . . and we have come to honor him."

A gaggle of curious onlookers murmured at this, but the soldier only grinned. "King of the Jews? There is but one king in Judea. If you'd like an audience with him, I'm sure I can arrange it."

Melchior lowered his head in a respectful bow. "My companions and I would be most grateful."

Herod ran a brush down the black Arabian's forelock, then stroked the stallion's bony jawline. The animal was nearly as imposing as Herod himself, a worthy addition to the royal stables.

He turned as Antipas and Tero entered, their faces flushed. "Well?" Herod lifted a brow. "Who are they?"

Antipas spoke first. "They are magi, from the East. The eldest, a man called Melchior, is a rab-mag."

Herod frowned. Why would men from the priestly caste of the Magians travel from Babylonia to Jerusalem? And why now? He tossed the brush to a groom and walked away from the horse. "What do they want?"

Tero bowed before answering. "If it please the king, they've come a great distance, bearing news you will want to hear. It's news—"

"They're claiming," Antipas interrupted, "the fulfillment of Daniel's prophecy."

"The sixty-nine weeks," Tero added. "You can call any rabbi; he will explain it to you."

Herod resisted the surge of fury that murmured in his ear. Did Tero think him a complete idiot? In truth, he knew little of Daniel and nothing of sixty-nine weeks, but he'd cut off Antipas's toes before he'd admit his ignorance before one of the Hebrew priests. He jerked his chin at his counselor. "You will bring me these men."

Tero cocked a brow. "Here? To the stable?"

"The reception area in the gardens," Herod answered, ripping out the words. "I will show these magi who reigns in Judea."

chapter twenty-eight

As the first shadows of night drifted over the eastern plain, Joseph pressed on, eager to reach Bethlehem before the watchmen closed the city gates. Mary had fallen silent on the donkey. He wondered if she dozed, until he heard the sound of a quiet cough.

A cough—not a good sound. He glanced over his shoulder, saw her huddled beneath her mantle, and glimpsed her drawn face. She could not ride much farther.

He looked ahead and saw a glimmer of light by the side of the road. Another shepherd, an old man, sat in front of a small fire, but he would have nothing to offer.

Joseph intended to nod and continue walking, but the old man spoke to him. "Your woman is cold."

With an eye on the disappearing sun, Joseph ignored the comment; then he heard Mary's voice. "Just for a moment? Can we . . . stop?"

They stopped. Joseph helped Mary from the donkey and watched, anxious about the late hour, as she held her hands before the crackling fire. A few feet away, a sheep bleated from within its protective hedge of stones and piled brush.

From out of the twilight gloom, a lamb appeared at Mary's side, seeking the warmth of her cloak.

The old man leaned forward. "Go on now. You already have a warm coat."

The lamb bleated again and scampered away.

"The little ones." The shepherd linked his hands. "They slip through the cracks, you know. That one got herself lost only yesterday. I was lucky to find her."

Joseph waited by the donkey and studied Mary's face as she lowered her hands and smiled. "I will tell our child about you," she said, daring to touch the shepherd's shoulder. "About your kindness."

The weather-beaten man only stared into the fire, but as Mary returned to Joseph, he spoke again. "My father told me long ago that we are all given something. A gift." The old man smiled as fire shadows lit his face. "Your gift is what you carry inside."

"And what," Mary answered, "is yours?"

The old man shook his head. "Nothing. Nothing but the hope of waiting for one."

Joseph extended his hand toward his wife. "We must go. If we're to reach Bethlehem by dark, we need to hurry."

Mary looked at him with compassion in her eyes. "You need to rest."

"I can rest in Bethlehem."

He was afraid she would disagree, but she accepted his hand and let him lead the way.

chapter twenty-nine

Melchior shot a look at Gaspar as a company of guards escorted the magi into Herod's palace. The Judean king had developed a reputation for building, but he had outdone himself in this city. The palace and its battlements dominated the skyline. Not even the ancient Babylonians had built on such a lavish, self-aggrandizing scale.

The thin, clean-shaven man sent to escort them into the king's presence introduced himself as Tero. With a tuft of silver hair spilling onto his forehead, he explained that he was the king's chief counselor and he'd been ordered to bring the magi directly to the gardens. When Melchior expressed his appreciation for Herod's palace, Tero proceeded to heap praise upon his master's accomplishments.

"There are two huge reception halls," the counselor said, leading them from the courtyard where they had left their camels, "and many bedrooms and courtyards—more than I have been able to count. Most notable are the three marble towers you must have noticed—Phasael, Hippicus, and Mariamne."

Melchior blinked. "Only a blind man would not notice the towers. But . . . the king *named* them?"

"After the dead." Tero lowered his voice. "Do not mention them unless the king does. Phasael, the king's brother, will forever be in Herod's favor, but Mariamne . . . though beloved by the king, she ran afoul of his temper and was executed. Hippicus, the king's friend, died in battle."

After leading them through several marble hallways decorated at regular intervals by golden statues, Tero gestured to an archway that opened to a garden. Melchior glanced at Gaspar and Balthasar, gave them a *be careful* look, and walked through the arch and down a garden path.

The garden was one of the finest he had ever seen. Cobblestone paths wound artfully between mounds of blue, yellow, and white flowers that trembled in the heat and exuded sweet perfume. A fountain provided the music of falling water and attracted dragonflies, which flashed in the air like shimmering gems.

Melchior was so taken with the gardens that he nearly didn't notice the old and heavyset man sitting on a padded bench in a clearing. Fortunately, Gaspar's abrupt cough reminded Melchior to bend his head and knee.

Herod, ruler of Judea, did not look much like a king. Short and heavy, his low brow did not indicate intelligence, and the curve of his lips offered more sneer than smile. But he extended a warm royal greeting to his guests, then gestured to several stands holding platters of bread, cheese, and cups of wine.

"You have come a long way." Herod's dark eyes sparked with curiosity. "Please, esteemed magi, let me honor you with the best my kingdom can offer. Eat, drink, and let me know how I can serve you."

Melchior bowed but did not move toward the tempting platters. "You are most kind, King Herod. We have come a long way, and we appreciate your thoughtful consideration. Our mission is simple but of the utmost importance." He gave Gaspar a confidential smile as he admitted, "I have waited a lifetime for this opportunity."

Herod glanced at his counselor, then pressed his elbow into the armrest of his bench. "Tero tells me you have been studying certain prophecies regarding the Hebrews."

"Many prophecies, Your Excellency, from many prophets. We have reason to believe the Hebrew Messiah will soon arrive. We have come to honor him."

He watched as Herod's mouth twisted in something not quite a smile. "And where will you find this Messiah?"

Melchior pressed his hands together. "We have come here, to Jerusalem, because the prophets say the king will reign from this holy city." He paused. "You, Herod, have been blessed with many years, as have I. Surely you understand that the time is right for a new king to rise."

Herod went pale as deep red patches appeared on his face, as though someone had slapped him hard on both cheeks. He snapped his fingers at his counselor. "Tero!"

The thin man stepped forward, adjusting the fold of the toga over his arm. "Excellency?"

"These men are searching for the Messiah . . . in Jerusalem."

Melchior tilted his head and watched as the king's counselor went a shade paler. "But . . . that's impossible," Tero stammered. "We have men—well, we would know if a king were gathering supporters in Jerusalem."

Herod pressed his lips together, then drew a deep breath and looked at his counselor with cunning in his eyes. "Call the rabbis and the leading priests, the teachers of religious law. Ask them where the Messiah will appear."

As Tero hurried to obey his master's bidding, Herod smiled in a way that only emphasized that he hadn't truly been smiling before. "Please—" he extended a jeweled hand—"eat, drink, and amuse yourself in my gardens. When I have an answer, I will share it with you."

"These—" Gaspar held up a fried locust—"are the best appetizers I have ever tasted. You must ask Tero how they are cooked."

Melchior was about to reply that he'd come about more important matters, but the sound of an approaching entourage distracted him. He elbowed Gaspar and cleared his throat to catch Balthasar's attention. The astronomer put down the wine he'd been sampling and came forward to stand beside his companions.

The magi waited as Herod swept into the garden, followed by guards, his counselor, and a half dozen men wearing the robes and phylacteries of Pharisees. The latter group frowned at the magi but said nothing.

Herod sat on his gilded bench, crossed his legs at the ankle, and gestured toward the religious leaders. "Ask them," he said, his gaze meeting Melchior's. "Ask them where this Messiah will be found."

Melchior turned but did not need to ask the question.

At the king's prodding, the eldest of the Pharisees stepped forward and began to translate a scroll. "The prophet Micah wrote, 'But you, O Bethlehem Ephrathah, are only a small village in Judah. Yet a ruler of Isra'el will come from you, one whose origins are from the distant past. The people of Isra'el will be abandoned to their enemies until the time when the woman in labor gives birth to her son. Then at last his fellow countrymen will return from exile to their own land. And he will stand to lead his flock with ADONAI's strength, in the majesty of the name of ADONAI his God. Then his people will live there undisturbed, for he will be highly honored all around the world. And he will be the source of our peace.'"

"Peace . . . from a man born in poor little Bethlehem?" Herod's mouth curled; then he gaped at Melchior like a man faced with a hard sum. "Are you not seeking a leader ready to proclaim himself Messiah?"

"Not a man," Balthasar stressed. "There are yet many years before he will reveal himself. We are seeking a *child* born for the lowest of men to the highest of kings. We have brought gifts and intend to pay him homage."

He smiled and Herod returned his smile, but with a distracted, inward look, as though he were thinking about something that had nothing to do with the present conversation.

A moment later the king's gaze sharpened. "When did you first see this sign in the heavens?"

Melchior turned to Balthasar. "How long, exactly?"

Balthasar frowned. "We first noticed the conjunction of the planets . . . nearly two years ago. A sign to alert us to the great event about to happen."

Melchior bowed. "Two years ago."

Herod rubbed his upper lip with a fat finger. "I too," he said, looking at Melchior, "have been waiting for God's Messiah. Ask any of the Jews; they will tell you I am sympathetic to their problems. I have rebuilt their Temple. I have taken pains not to offend them. Did you notice that I have not placed my image on the coins of the realm? Graven images offend the Jews . . . and I would do nothing to offend them."

He leaned forward, propping one elbow upon a flabby knee, and lowered his voice to a conspiratorial tone. "Trust me, esteemed friends—like you, I am a true seeker of God. So go to Bethlehem and search for this child. When you have found him, return to me and bring word of his whereabouts . . . so I may go and honor him as well."

Melchior bowed, as did Gaspar and Balthasar. Tero strode forward to escort them back to their camels, but Melchior couldn't resist turning to catch a last glimpse of Herod.

The king was berating the assembled religious leaders, his face an alarming shade of red.

"I don't like it," Melchior murmured as they passed the fountain.

Gaspar's brows knit together. "What don't you like? The king seems forthright in his intentions. The people do speak of his forbearance with the Hebrews."

Aware that he walked in a place filled with listening ears, Melchior did not respond. As they walked back to the stable, Melchior did not examine the garden but found himself studying the magnificent square tower Herod had named Mariamne, in honor of the beautiful queen he had adored . . . and murdered.

Mary bent lower, her head nearly touching the donkey's bobbing neck. She had been experiencing a dull sort of throbbing ache since they left Jerusalem, but now the pain seemed to intensify with every step. She tried to distract herself by fitting words to the donkey's rhythmic step.

Soon we will stop, and we will be blessed. Soon we will stop, oh, soon we will rest—

She gasped as pain rose inside her like a wave, crashing, sending rivulets of agony through her belly, her back, her limbs.

Joseph turned, his brows drawing together. "Mary?"

She held her breath, braced herself against the hurt, and slowly exhaled.

"Joseph," she gasped. Then the agony struck again.

chapter thirty

The sight of Mary's anguish threatened to freeze Joseph's scalp to his skull. He brought his hand down on the donkey's rump, sending the animal into a startled trot. He ran alongside, realizing too late that the animal's jouncing might aggravate Mary's discomfort.

"We will find a shelter. I promise," he said, catching his breath between phrases. "There will be many to help in the village ahead. I will find a midwife and women—"

He glanced at Mary, who clung to the donkey's mane with both hands, her face pale, her forehead streaked with sweat. Her legs, which she usually kept modestly tucked beneath the edge of her tunic, hung limply at the beast's side, as if she lacked the energy to lift them.

Joseph stared at his wife's sandaled foot and wondered if ADONAI had made a grave mistake in calling him to this responsibility.

High in his padded saddle, Melchior looked to his right and studied the western horizon. The sun stood balanced upon the line where the land met the heavens, and already a few stars sparkled against the smoky dome of twilight. "Balthasar," he called, "what think you of the sky?"

Balthasar peered at the horizon for only a moment, then pulled a star chart from one of his saddlebags. "Trouble," he announced after a moment of consideration. "Mercury, Venus, Mars, Jupiter, and the moon are clustered in Leo-Virgo."

"So?"

"War is on the way. Certain destruction."

Melchior grunted. War . . . earthly or heavenly? He knew of no strife stirring Judea, so this might be a war in the heavenlies . . . or it could mean nothing.

His camel lifted her head and quickened her pace, probably realizing that rest and a manger of sweet hay waited at the end of the road. As the beast stretched her legs, Melchior studied the outline of the village that lay directly south. Bethlehem, a mere outpost of Jerusalem, did not have much size to recommend it, but Tero said it had been the birthplace of David, Israel's greatest king.

Melchior had felt the truth hit him like a blow. Why had he assumed that the Messiah would be born in David's capital? The root of David, the branch from David's line, should be born in the village of David's birth.

Darkness pushed against the eastern sky like a beast prowling the night, but orange and red and purple light still streaked the west. Melchior watched as the sun slid from sight and a jumble of stars glittered against the charcoal sky. Finally *the* star arose, right where it should be. The glittering orb hung low in the southeastern sky, sparkling like a diamond against velvet. It would follow its orbit in the heavens, traveling up and over Judea until it set shortly before sunrise. . . .

Perhaps by then they would have an answer.

He was about to share his thoughts with Gaspar and Balthasar when the star *moved*. Not in its course, not as it should have. The star, still burning bright, was coming *down* the sky, turning southward, as if it meant to lead them like a gleaming beacon.

He blinked, not trusting his eyes, but Balthasar's cry affirmed his senses. "Melchior! Do you see?"

Melchior jangled his reins and burst into song as the camel carried him forward.

❧

Since the time of Abraham, when he offered food and drink to angelic visitors, the children of Isra'el had been enjoined to extend hospitality to strangers. On any other night, Joseph could have taken Mary to the well, where eventually someone would have offered them a place to rest in their home.

This was not an ordinary night.

Joseph felt an icy finger touch the base of his spine as he neared the gates of Bethlehem. The Romans had erected *katalumas*, or temporary shelters, around the city walls. The shelters consisted of little more than open tents, and all were overflowing with people and livestock. Nowhere could Joseph find room for himself and Mary.

Yet Bethlehem still had a well and his people still had a tradition. He pushed through the crowd, steeling himself to the sound of Mary's muffled cries, dragging the donkey when he balked in the press of people and animals and soldiers. Joseph pushed and prodded until they entered the sagging gates of Bethlehem; then he led the donkey down a largely deserted street until they reached the well at the marketplace. There he helped Mary dismount and held her hand while he looked around.

No one came to offer assistance—no one even walked the streets. The presence of so many Romans and strangers outside the city must have intimidated the local people, for they had disappeared like shadows.

He turned and squeezed Mary's hands. "I have to go find help."

"Joseph." Her voice was fainter than air. "Don't leave me."

"I'll be back. I promise. Wait here and I'll find help." He squeezed her hands a final time and turned, afraid to look at her again. If he looked into her eyes and saw pain, he wouldn't be able to leave her, not ever.

He ran to the closest house and pounded on the door.

A man opened it a crack, looked Joseph up and down.

"My wife," Joseph begged, "please, she is with child. We need—"

"Sorry." The man was already closing the door. "We have no room and nothing to spare."

"I beg you." Joseph braced his hand on the wood, testing its strength with his arm. If necessary, he could—he *would*—break it down. "Please," he said again, calming himself, "we mean you no harm. My wife is having her pains; her time of travail has come. We need a place to shelter. She needs a midwife—"

The door opened wider, caught by another hand, and Joseph found himself staring into the impassive brown eyes of a woman. "I'm sorry," she said, her voice flat. "But as you can see, we have nothing to spare."

Joseph would have protested, but a single glance at the room proved the woman's words. The house, smoky with the family's cook fire, was crowded with bodies and heavy with the odors of people and animals. The family goat and two sheep stood in one corner; three elders sat in a huddle while a half dozen children lay shoulder to shoulder on straw-stuffed pallets.

Joseph swallowed his protests. "I'm sorry to disturb you. If you can tell me where I could find a midwife—"

"Any woman that's had a child of her own can help," the wife answered, shrugging. "Nothing to it, truly. Just pray the babe is born alive."

And as the door closed, a new fear crept into Joseph's soul. What if the journey, the rush, the rough handling—what if all of it had done something to injure the babe Mary carried?

What sort of curse befalls a man who kills the only begotten Son of God?

Though Mary clung to the donkey's mane and tried not to follow Joseph's conversation, she couldn't help overhearing the woman's words. A thousand nameless fears swarmed out of the darkness and surrounded her, mingling with her pain, exhaustion, and dark memories of her sister-in-law's travails.

What if the baby was stillborn? Such things happened all the time. Sometimes the baby died, sometimes the mother. And sometimes the baby lived a day or two before it took a last struggling breath and closed its eyes.

Perhaps ADONAI meant for her to deliver this child and close her eyes forever. After all, Gabriel hadn't promised that she'd live to raise her miracle son, and the strange prophet on the street had said a sword would pierce her soul. . . .

As Joseph ran from house to house, beating on door after door with the same fevered plea, Mary realized her baby would be born in the city of Bethlehem, the poorest, most crowded village they had yet entered.

"ADONAI," Mary breathed, lifting her eyes to the starry sky, "be with your servant now."

In the field outside Bethlehem, Ozni, the old shepherd, threw a stick on his fire, settled the lamb on his lap, and watched as a caravan of camels passed on the road. Men from the East, judging from the colorful turbans and silk robes they wore. Rich men, probably, for even their pack camels jingled with adornment.

One of them rode with a smile on his lined face, intent on the town ahead. The second man rode with an instrument in his hand, a circular object that gleamed in the silver light of the moon. The third man hunched in his saddle, looking as bored as an eel sorter at the fish market.

Ozni waited until the last camel had passed, then tossed another stick on his fire and drew the lamb closer to his breast. "Fine folk like that will have nothing to do with us—" he nuzzled the wee beast under the chin—"so we have no need to worry about them."

Mary released a groan as the round ball of her belly pressed against the sweaty donkey. Her legs felt like straw; she wondered if they would continue to hold her weight. The stabbing pains came more regularly now, each one more distinct and urgent than the one before. Her tunic was saturated with sweat, her cheeks wet with tears.

And Joseph had . . . vanished.

He had disappeared down the closest street, working his way from house to house until she lost sight of him. The sun had deserted the western horizon, leaving her with only an attenuated moon and a few stars for light. Few lamps burned in the windows of Bethlehem, for even olive oil was a luxury in this threadbare village.

She had come from Nazareth, left home and family, comfort and warmth, to find herself in agony and . . . alone.

Mary gripped the donkey's mane with both hands as grief welled within her, black and cold. "Why?" She lifted her running eyes to the distant stars. "Why would you bring me so far to abandon me now? Please . . . will you not provide for us?"

Nothing answered in the dark night—not ADONAI, not Gabriel, not some lesser angel.

Not even Joseph.

chapter thirty-one

By the light of a clay lamp in Juttah, Elizabeth splashed warm water on her perfect six-month-old son, then lifted him from the basin. He reached for her nose as she set him on clean linen, and she laughed as she scrubbed his stocky body dry.

"Now you are clean, my big boy." She kept her voice low so not to disturb her dozing husband. "The dust of another day is washed away."

The baby slapped his hands together; then his smile faded. A strange, faintly eager look flashed in his eyes, a look so odd and unchildlike that Elizabeth paused.

"Zechariah," she called, not caring if she woke him, "come quickly."

The expression had vanished by the time Zechariah reached her side, but Elizabeth tried to explain as she laid her son between their pallets. "I know it sounds crazy, but John looked at me as if . . . he *knew* something."

Zechariah chuckled, his hand finding hers in the semidarkness. "And what could a baby know?"

"I don't know, but didn't the angel tell you he would be filled with the Ruach HaKodesh even before his birth? I tell you, Husband, the Spirit of ADONAI has revealed something to him."

Elizabeth lowered her face and stared into her infant's wide eyes. "What is it?"

Driven by rising panic, Joseph sprinted down the street where he'd left Mary. His heart stopped when he didn't see her beside the donkey, but it resumed beating double time when he spied her huddled against the side of the well. She was still counting on him, still holding on.

He beat on the last door, a large house opposite the place where he'd begun, and started speaking the moment the door opened a crack. "Please. My wife is about to give birth and there is no one to help us."

The man—a short fellow so thick that his head appeared to rest directly on his shoulders—opened the door wider, his eyes narrowing when he saw Mary.

"I beg you," Joseph continued, not caring if the man realized the extent of his desperation. "I ask not for room in your house but any shelter you have. Any bit of shelter, but we need a place where she can lie down and have a woman help her."

The man hesitated, then turned to whisper to someone behind the door.

With a small clay lamp held high, the short man led Joseph's donkey down an alley and into the holding pen for his animals. A pair of goats shuffled nervously as they approached; a mule flicked its ears, then returned to his doze.

The stable lacked four walls, but a rocky overhang formed a roof of sorts and would provide shelter in case of rain. The back of the house would block the wind, and the place offered an abundance of straw for Mary's bed.

The man, who had introduced himself as Thomas, waited until Joseph helped Mary sit on a bale of hay before handing him the lamp. "I'm sorry, but this is all I have to offer."

Joseph took the lamp and gave the man a heartfelt smile. "We thank you. If you know of a midwife—"

"Bethlehem had a midwife," Thomas answered. "Dorcas. But she died yesterday."

Joseph groaned, his heart thumping almost painfully in his chest. "Please. My wife is about to have a child and I don't know—I've never—"

"Any woman would know what to do." The merchant looked away from Mary, who was clinging to a fence rail. "I'd send my wife, but she's busy tending to our guests. You can go try to find a woman who will come out with you—"

"Joseph." Mary's voice, though exhausted, rang with iron. "Don't go."

⚜

When the merchant left them, Mary looked at her husband through a veil of tears. He had found her a place. He had secured a lamp. They were safe and dry and no longer on the road.

"Mary." Joseph knelt beside her and took her hand. "I don't know how to do this. I've never been in the same room with a woman giving birth. I'm a carpenter, not a farmer, so I've never even—"

"I need you," she said simply, looking into his eyes. "I was with Elizabeth. I witnessed her child's birth. I think . . . I *know* we will be all right. But I will need your help."

She reached up, pulled her dusty veil from her head, and gave it to him. "Shake it off; make it as clean as you can. See if you can find another cloth and tear it into strips. And—" she gritted her teeth against another pain—"see if you can find something to serve as a bed for the child. We can't have him being trampled by the goats or the donkey."

He rose to do her bidding, and Mary pushed herself upright. She wanted nothing more than to curl up in a bed of hay and sleep, but first she had work to do.

And God would have to supply the strength for her labor.

The old shepherd glanced up as a hooting owl fluttered onto the branch of an olive tree. The sky, which had been quiet and calm, now glimmered with the light of a dozen stars. The sparkling orb that had shone in the southeast had come down like the shekinah glory that once led Isra'el through the desert. It hovered over the road between the caravan and Bethlehem and seemed to turn, growing more brilliant and bright with every rotation.

The hair at the back of Ozni's neck rose with premonition. Was this a miracle . . . or an omen?

Melchior's eyes widened as the star twisted and sparked overhead. Beside him, Balthasar's feathery brows shot up to his hairline, and Gaspar's face went idiotic with astonishment.

"This is not a conjunction of stars," Balthasar said, speaking in a hushed voice. "This is . . ."

". . . the work of God," Melchior finished. "This is beyond anything the skies have ever displayed. This is a marvel meant for us, a sign that we have done well to search for this king."

For the first time, Gaspar had no disparaging comment. He simply watched the wonder, then whispered, "Can it be true?"

"It is," Melchior said, urging his camel to follow the blazing beacon.

Mary lay on her side, the red ribbon tight in her fist. Joseph ran a damp cloth over her head and begged ADONAI to give them strength for the hour ahead.

A sudden stab caused Mary to cry out. She pressed her lips together and breathed through her nose, struggling to think not of the pain but of the miracle about to be born. . . .

Unable to sleep with a restless infant, Elizabeth lifted her swaddled baby and stepped into the moonlit courtyard in search of fresh air. In the heavy quiet of the night, the baby cooed in her arms and batted her face with a tiny fist. She laughed softly and lifted him in her arms, then gasped as his dark eyes filled with brilliance.

What was this?

When the baby smiled and stared at something in the distance, Elizabeth realized she was seeing the reflection of something in the night sky. She turned and saw a sparkling star descending from the heavens and shining a beam of light toward Jerusalem.

No . . . toward Bethlehem.

She felt the truth all at once, like a tingle in the pit of her stomach. In a voice brimming with wonder, she whispered, "So that's where you are, Cousin. In Bethlehem . . . giving birth to my Lord."

And then, with her baby in her arms, Elizabeth twirled in the silence of the night and sang the words of the prophet Isaiah: "'Do not tremble; do not be afraid. Have I not proclaimed from ages past what my purposes are for you? Sing for joy, O heavens! Rejoice, O earth! For ADONAI has comforted his people.'"

"Now." Mary panted and reached for Joseph's hand. "Help me up, now."

He reached for her, steadied her arms, and helped her find her footing on the packed earthen floor. He had scraped some clean straw together, forming a rude nest, and Mary lowered herself over it.

When he knelt before her, she gripped his shoulders. "I'm going to push," she said, her eyes almost disappearing as her face clenched in great effort. "You catch the baby."

Joseph blinked. How was he supposed to do this?

He watched, his gut straining with sympathetic effort, until Mary gasped and a head emerged from between her trembling limbs.

He spread his fingers and felt a warm, wet tide splash over his palms, followed by a pink bundle of baby.

Joseph stared at the miracle in his work-worn hands. For an instant his mind went blank, overcome with feelings and thoughts too unfathomable to shape into words.

After drawing and releasing a deep breath, Mary sat back on the straw and nodded at the pulsing cord that still connected her to her son. "You'll have to cut it and tie it off." She gave Joseph a look that clearly said *don't panic.* "Measure a finger's length from the child's belly and make the cut there."

He did as she instructed, using a flint to cut the flesh and tying off the bloody stump with a piece of string from his garment.

"Wash him," Mary whispered, leaning back on her elbows as if she no longer had the strength to sit upright. "Wrap him in the strips you tore. Wrap him tight against the chill. . . . Then you can bring him to me."

Joseph washed the child with water from the animals' trough. The infant in his hands had dark, wet hair, long lashes, a tiny nose, and small, perfect lips. He flailed sweet, soft arms, kicked feet crowned with stubby toes, and stared at Joseph with eyes that seemed to look straight into his soul. . . .

What do you see, little one? A man worthy of your trust?

When Joseph had managed everything Mary had asked, he took the baby to his wife and watched as she set the infant on her sweat-stained clothing. Tears trickled down her cheeks as she opened her tunic and began to nurse the child of God, born for mankind.

Joseph didn't realize he was weeping until he tasted the salt of his tears.

Out in the shepherd's field, the tiny lamb scampered away from her guardian. Ozni felt the animal go but he didn't react, so intent was he on the pinwheeling celestial wonder above the road to Bethlehem.

"By all that is holy," he murmured, wishing for the soul of a priest or a poet, someone who could combine words to adequately depict the glorious sight, "would you look at that?"

He shifted as a gust of wind blew past him, then glanced at the wandering lamb. The wee beast had stopped, its head tracking the movement of something at Ozni's left. He turned, half expecting to see an approaching traveler, but a stranger stood on the side of the road.

A stranger unlike any man Ozni had ever seen.

He shrank back, the skin on his forearms pebbling with goose-flesh, as the man radiated with living light.

"Don't be afraid," the stranger said, "I bring you good news of great joy . . . for *everyone*."

Ozni felt his throat tighten. Good news was never meant for out-casts like him. Like animals, he and his kind lived outdoors, forbidden to enter the Temple, a synagogue, or a decent family's dwelling.

The stranger's hair gleamed in the light of the dazzling star. "For everyone," he repeated. "The Savior—yes, the Messiah, the Lord—has been born tonight in Bethlehem, the City of David. And this is how you will recognize him: You will find a baby lying in a manger, wrapped snugly in strips of cloth."

Ozni watched in wonder as the wind blew again and the stranger vanished as suddenly as he had appeared.

The shepherd took a step back and lowered his gaze. He had spent his life waiting for the gift his father once promised, and perhaps it had come. . . . Well, *certainly* it had come. An angel had appeared and personally delivered news that would change the world.

Or was this all a dream?

The old man took a hesitant step toward the city. Beside him, the little lamb bleated, and the sound restored Ozni's sense of reality. This was *real*, this was his world, for at his feet stood a living lamb.

"All right, then." He bent and scooped the animal into his arms. "Hate to lose me, do you?"

In his vulnerable, crouched position, Ozni sensed movement in the night. With his nerves at a full stretch, he turned, expecting to find an intruder in the fold, but the sheep stood undisturbed. Behind him, however, on the surrounding hilltops where dozens of other shepherds had settled their flocks for the night, other men stood with awestruck faces and looked toward Bethlehem. The star's silver light bathed them all in radiance.

In that moment Ozni understood—the angel's message had been for every shepherd in the vicinity.

They, the outcasts of Isra'el, had been invited to witness a miracle.

Melchior, Gaspar, and Balthasar let their camels pick their way through a pack of barking dogs that darted in and out of the otherwise quiet katalumas. The transients who had crowded into the shelters slept now, their eyes closed to the spectacle glittering over the drowsing town of Bethlehem.

The gates of the city loomed before the magi, open and unattended. One of the wooden gates hung crooked on its hinges; obviously it had not been closed for some time.

"Not very vigilant, these people," Balthasar remarked. "Anyone could come in and steal anything."

Gaspar shifted in his saddle. "From the look of this place, I think it's safe to say these people have few treasures worthy of being stolen. Look at these mean huts, these scrawny animals."

"And so the city sleeps," Melchior murmured as his mount passed through the gate, "unaware of the honor bestowed upon it."

He kicked his camel, urging the old girl into the streets of Bethlehem.

Like most ancient cities, the place of David's birth was an amalgamation of winding streets, hidden alleys, and crowded structures. Melchior would have despaired of ever finding the right place, but the extraordinary star did not fail to lead the way. The celestial orb went before them, guiding them with a cylindrical beam that led them down a narrow street and past a crumbling well. It stopped before a house, clearly lighting the wooden door.

Melchior gave his camel the command to kneel and clung to his saddle as the beast went down on her front knees, then settled her hindquarters on the earth. Gaspar and Balthasar also dismounted, their faces taut with expectation.

Gaspar reached Melchior first. "Surely this is the wrong place. This house is not worthy of a king."

Melchior studied the light blazing directly overhead. "Would you protest against the star that has led us so far?"

Balthasar walked up, stiff and limping from his hours in the saddle. "Surely there's been some mistake. Perhaps we are seeking a house behind this one, a place hidden from our sight."

"We will inquire here." Melchior knocked on the door. He waited, his hands clasped in front of him, for an interval that seemed woven of eternity. Finally he heard fumbling.

"Excuse me for disturbing you," he said, bowing when the door opened, "but we have come here seeking a child."

The short man at the door frowned up at the sky. "What's that?"

"A star." Melchior calmly folded his hands. "As I said, we are looking for a child. Perhaps a baby."

The man squinted into the light, then grunted and jerked his thumb toward the side of the house. "Out back, through the alley. The only baby at this house would be in the stable."

Melchior blinked at the man in dazed exasperation. "The stable, you said?"

The man closed the door, leaving Melchior staring at a panel of rough-hewn wood.

Gaspar shook his head. "Inexplicable, all of it. Surely this is some kind of mistake—"

Melchior cut him off with an upraised hand. "Would we come so far only to turn away because the baby is in an unlikely place?"

Accompanied by the crunching steps of his companions, he drew his robe closer around him and walked through the alley that ran along the side of the house. He glimpsed the wooden rails of a fence, saw the profile of a mule with its back leg bent in relaxed sleep, heard the ninny of goats. He breathed in the scents of manure and hay as he rounded the corner.

And then he glimpsed the top of a woman's head. "Have no fear," he murmured, lifting his hand to stop his friends. "This is the place."

With a confidence born of faith, Melchior hurried back to the camels. He pulled the casket containing his gift from his saddlebags, brushed the dust from his robe, and smoothed his beard. When he was certain his appearance displayed the respect necessary to approach royalty, he tucked the gilded casket beneath his arm and led the way back to the stable.

What he saw there stole his breath away. An infant king, bareheaded and tiny, suckling the breast of a girl young enough to be Melchior's granddaughter. A life so fragile and new it could be extinguished with the flick of a blade or a single blow.

A baby . . . in a stable.

A bearded man stepped forward, his hands fisted and his eyes blazing. Without being told, Melchior knew this man would do anything to protect the mother and child.

"Pray excuse us." Melchior bowed his head and lowered his knee to the ground. "We have journeyed many days and come a long way . . . to honor the newborn king."

The young mother looked up and modestly covered herself as the baby stilled in sleep.

The bearded man hesitated, then took the child from her and placed the infant in a bed he'd fashioned of straw.

A king . . . in a manger.

"I see him," Melchior whispered, "in this present time. I perceive him, but not where we expected. A star has risen from Jacob; a scepter has emerged from Israel."

The bearded man threw him a sharp look, wariness in his eyes.

Melchior swept his turban from his head. "I beg you, forgive our intrusion, but we have been following the star. It has led us to this house, to you."

The man glanced at the sky, and his hand went protectively to the woman's shoulder. She smiled at Melchior, her eyes shining despite the lines of weariness on her face.

"As befits a king, we have brought gifts." Melchior pulled the gilded casket from beneath his arm and set it before the child's mother, then lifted the lid. "A gift of gold, for the King of kings."

Balthasar stepped up beside him, knelt, and produced his present. "A pot of frankincense, for the Priest of all priests."

Gaspar spoke with quiet conviction. "A gift of myrrh," he said, setting an alabaster jar with the other containers, "to honor your sacrifice."

Melchior waited in silence as the mother looked at the gifts, then reached for her husband's hand.

The man shook his head. "I don't know what to say."

The mother looked at her sleeping child. "There are some things," she said, her voice slight and frail in the night, "for which we lack words and understanding. But thank you." She offered a smile to the magi. "For your gifts and for your faith."

Joseph, his nerves on full alert, looked up as another shadow crossed the hay. A man stood there, an old man he dimly recognized from some other time and place.

The little lamb he carried bleated, awakening the memory. "The shepherd," he said, as much for Mary's benefit as for his own. "From the road."

The wizened man dropped to his knees before the baby, then looked at Mary. "You." Wonder filled his eyes. "I remember you."

Joseph moved closer as the old man lowered his lamb to the straw and let his gaze drift to the child in the manger. He reached out as if he would stroke the baby's head, then withdrew his hand.

"It's all right." Mary nodded in encouragement. "He is for all mankind."

The shepherd placed his palm against the child's head, then trembled as a smile creased his face.

Behind him, the three visitors from the East watched in wonder.

Mary scooted closer to her sleeping baby and looked into the shepherd's face. "We are each given a gift."

The sound of soft footsteps caught Joseph's ear. He turned to find the alley crowded with more than a dozen shepherds who had come to pay homage to the child in a manger of Bethlehem.

When the unexpected guests had gone, Mary stretched out in the hay next to the manger. After one last check on her sleeping son, she lowered her head to her arm and closed her eyes.

Though her body cried out for rest, her heart and mind stirred with conflicting emotions. She had held her child in her arms and felt awe at the reality of God in flesh. One ought to tremble and bow before the Master of the Universe, but all she wanted to do was cover her son in kisses. Part of her wanted to kneel at the baby's feet and wait for ADONAI to guide and provide, yet another part of her yearned to care for Jesus, to bathe and clothe him, to sing in his ear and hold him close to her breast.

How was she to raise this Son of God?

What was she supposed to do when he got sick? *Would* he get sick? Would he stub his toe, skin his knees, cut his chin?

Would he cry with weariness and wail when he was hungry? Would he run to her arms when he needed comfort, or would he look to ADONAI?

Would she be a comfort to him . . . or a disappointment? For she was only a woman, prone to mistakes, too quick to worry, and sometimes too slow to reveal the deep affections of her heart.

Through a haze of exhaustion, she felt a blanket brush her shoulder. Joseph.

She opened her eyes and saw him standing beside the baby, keeping watch over both of them. "Are you well?" he asked, ever solicitous. "Do you need anything?"

Mary reached across the manger, caught his hand, and squeezed it. "I have been given the strength I prayed for. Strength from God . . . and from you."

chapter thirty-two

The first pale hints of sunrise were warming the eastern sky when the magi glimpsed the city walls of Jerusalem in the distance. Melchior called a halt and reigned in his camel. Gaspar rode up to join him, followed by Balthasar.

Melchior nodded at the guards who rode at the front and rear, signaling that he needed a moment to consult with his companions. He looked at the others.

Balthasar rubbed the back of his neck with his hand. Gaspar sat without speaking, his eyes still bright with their discovery.

Melchior couldn't stop a smile. After spending a mostly sleepless night sitting in the hay of a rustic stable, they ought to be dead tired and irritable. But how could one be irritated in the face of a living miracle?

After a moment of protracted silence, Gaspar's face split into a wide grin. "You're not going back to Herod, are you?"

Melchior leaned both arms on the pommel of his saddle and jerked his chin at Balthasar. "Tell me, friend—yesterday, what were you saying about war and destruction?"

The astronomer did not need to consult his star charts. "For the first time, Mars has entered the conjunction of sun, moon, Mercury, Venus, and Jupiter. Mars means war."

Melchior stroked his beard and considered Herod's marble city.

Perhaps God was warning him through the stars, or perhaps this conjunction meant nothing. But an uneasiness moved at the core of his being, and he hadn't liked the look of cunning he'd glimpsed in Herod's eye.

Last night he'd seen that same look in a dream he had while dozing next to some talkative shepherd. He, Gaspar, and Balthasar had been standing on a sandbar surrounded by snapping crocodiles wearing the look he's seen in Herod's eyes when he asked about the coming king.

"The one they call Herod the Great has murdered two sons and a wife," Melchior said, picking up his reins. "I do not think he'd hesitate to kill an innocent child of Bethlehem, do you?"

Neither Gaspar nor Balthasar answered, but neither did they protest when Melchior turned his camel away from Herod's city. They would take the road from Bethlehem to Jericho, heading east without returning to Jerusalem.

But they would never forget this journey.

Joseph awakened with a start. He lifted his head and checked on Mary and the baby. Mary was awake, curled at Joseph's side with the baby at her breast. She smiled at the child, wonder and love mingling in her eyes as she nursed.

Joseph took advantage of the silence to study his bride. He had been impressed by Mary's strength in Nazareth, but the difficult journey, the jolting ride, and the hard labor had taken their toll. Lines of strain bracketed her mouth while blue circles of exhaustion lay beneath her eyes.

She had left Nazareth a girl . . . and would return a woman.

When Joseph sat up, Mary gave him a smile he would accept as his last sight on earth. "Good morning, Husband. Did you sleep at all?"

"A little." He examined the baby, touched the tip of his finger to the child's perfect pink nose. "Are you well?"

"A little tired . . . and sore." She tilted her head toward the hay beyond. "Somehow I think our friends will not be so happy to awaken here."

Joseph chuckled as he followed her gaze. Most of the shepherds had returned to their flocks last night, but two boys—young men, really—had remained behind, probably lulled to sleep by the close quarters and the older men's stories.

Joseph crawled forward on his hands and knees and jiggled the foot of a sleeping youth. "Time to wake. The sun is up."

The young man lifted his head, blinked, and punched his companion. "Zedekiah! The flock!"

They rose and brushed straw from their tunics, blushing as they bid Joseph a hasty farewell. One of them bobbed in an awkward bow before the baby, then turned and sprinted through the alley.

Joseph sat beside Mary and hooked his arm around one bent knee. "I have to register," he said, thinking aloud, "and we need a place to stay until you can travel again."

"Don't worry about me—"

"Shh." Joseph cut her off with a smile. "A husband is *supposed* to worry about his wife. I will talk to the man who owns this stable; perhaps he knows where a carpenter can find a few days' work."

She nodded, and in her eyes he saw the soft light of gratitude.

"Well . . . I see a new life has entered the world."

Startled, Mary looked up to find Thomas and his wife at the entrance of the stable. Three little boys behind the woman peeped around her skirts.

Mary offered a wan smile while Joseph leaped to his feet. "We don't know how to thank you. We had no place to go, and the baby was coming—"

"I only wish we could have done more." The merchant tapped his wife's arm and began the introductions. "This is my wife, Deborah; my children, Eber, Eli, and Abel. We have good news—our guests are departing, so we would like you to stay inside with us."

Deborah crouched in the straw beside Mary. "This is not a fit place for a baby. Please, come inside the house. I have bread, milk, and dates to break your fast."

Mary glanced at Joseph. She would not have to be asked twice, so if he was agreeable . . .

He was. He helped Mary to her feet, thanked the family once again, and asked if anyone in the village had need of a skilled carpenter. "Though we came only for the registration, my wife will not want to travel for a while." He folded his hands. "I'd like to earn my keep while we're here."

Thomas grinned and slapped Joseph on the back. "If you hail from Bethlehem, my friend, you will find a cousin on every corner. Come inside, eat, and let me walk you through town. We will put you to work at once because a good carpenter is hard to find."

Mary counted off eight days, then reminded Joseph that their son must be circumcised according to the Law.

Joseph, who had not forgotten, mentioned the need for a rabbi, and Thomas sent straightaway for the old man who served their village.

With Mary, Thomas, Deborah, and their children as witnesses, the rabbi lifted the metal knife as Joseph held the baby. "Blessed be the Lord our God who has sanctified us by his precepts and has given us circumcision," the rabbi chanted, his voice as flat and dry as the desert. "As ADONAI commanded, 'He that is eight days old shall be circumcised among you . . . and my covenant shall be in your flesh for an everlasting covenant.'"

Mary closed her eyes as the sharp blade did its work, then comforted her crying baby by holding him close.

The rabbi ended the ceremony with the customary prayer: "May our God, and the God of our fathers, raise up this child to his father and mother, and let his name be called in Isra'el—" The old man halted and looked at Joseph. "What have you named him?"

"Jesus," Joseph answered, after a quick glance at Mary.

Jesus, meaning "ADONAI saves." For he shall save his people from their sins.

After receiving congratulations from Thomas and his family, Joseph drew Mary close, placed a kiss on her brow, and left the house with the stocky merchant. Thomas had decided to expand his booth in the marketplace, so he had hired Joseph to construct a new frame, a roof, and three walls high enough to prevent children from running between the merchant's feet.

Mary watched her husband go, then turned to help Deborah in the house. She could benefit from watching the older woman, for Thomas's wife had learned to balance the needs of her children, her husband's business, and the work of running a household.

Before lowering Jesus into his basket, Mary kissed her baby's cheek and thought of the miracle God had granted. She did not know how an unschooled village girl was supposed to guide the Son of God from infancy to maturity, but ADONAI had brought them safely thus far.

Surely he would continue to provide.

After forty sweet days in David's city, Mary walked the road between Bethlehem and Jerusalem once again. At her right and left, green pastures rippled in the wind and vibrated with insect life. She looked for the shepherds who had visited on the night of Jesus' birth, but they must have been feeding their flocks in meadows farther afield.

Though she and Joseph were glad to make this journey, they had little choice in the matter. According to the Law, Mary had been ceremonially unclean since the baby's birth. Until she had been ceremonially purified, she would be forbidden to touch any consecrated item or worship in a synagogue.

Furthermore, because all firstborns belonged to ADONAI, while they were at the Temple she and Joseph would also have to redeem their firstborn son according to the terms of the Law.

A blush burned her cheek when she considered their sacrifices.

Two turtledoves—the offering specified for a poor woman—would serve as Mary's purification offering, but the prescribed amount for the redemption of a firstborn son was five silver shekels—an amount they would not have had if not for the magi's gracious gifts.

ADONAI had provided everything they needed.

After walking the six miles to Jerusalem, they entered the Holy City and walked through the winding streets that led to the Temple. Mary recognized several familiar landmarks. To her right lay the street of the academies, where wealthy families sent their sons to study Torah with esteemed teachers of the Law. Straight ahead lay the bridge that led to the Royal Porch and the Court of the Gentiles.

As always, the unusual sights and sounds of the city fascinated Mary, but a curt comment from Joseph caught her attention. "This"— her husband spoke in a low growl—"used to be a holy place."

Surprised, she glanced around to see what had upset him. Joseph was looking into the Court of the Gentiles, which roiled with activity. Money changers sat at tables while herdsmen offered livestock to be used in the sacrifices. Within and without the court, men bartered and bargained in voices so loud she could hear some of them arguing from where she stood.

"Come." Joseph pressed his hand to her back. "We must attend to our business."

With that less-than-holy vision of the outer court still playing in her mind, Mary and Joseph entered the Temple. In the Court of the Women, Mary walked up to one of the trumpet-shaped offering chests and deposited the price of a pair of turtledoves. She waited until the voice of the magrephah announced that incense was about to be offered in the Holy Place; then she looked for the station man, a lay representative of Isra'el, who would tell her what to do next.

The station man directed her and several other women to the top of the fifteen steps that led from the Court of the Women to the Court of Isra'el. Mary's heart thumped against her rib cage, for she had never stood so close to the Holy Place. As the worshippers' prayers rose and the attending priests entered the room containing the golden altar, she glanced at the joy-filled faces of the daughters of Isra'el around her and joined them in giving thanks to ADONAI for keeping her safe through the risks and rigors of childbirth.

When the prayers had been offered, the incense burned, and the drink offerings poured out, Mary found Joseph in the crowd. Together they went to a priest and presented their firstborn son.

The priest stepped forward and placed his hand on the child's head, offering a perfunctory benediction in a disinterested voice.

When he had finished, Mary held the baby as Joseph paid the price for their son's redemption. She couldn't stop a wry smile—did the priest realize what he was witnessing? Joseph was obediently redeeming the Son who had no need of redemption, for Jesus would *be* God, always and forever.

Yet not every priest was blind to the truth. Joseph had no sooner returned to Mary's side than an old cohen, a *tzaddik*, lifted his hand and called out a greeting from across the court. He walked with an urgency that belied his years, and the face beneath his head covering gleamed with awe.

"Do you know him?" Mary whispered as the old man approached with long, purposeful strides.

Joseph shook his head. "I've never seen him before."

The aging priest took one look at the child in Mary's arms and clapped his hands. "Praise ADONAI," he shouted, apparently not caring who heard. "Now I can die in peace!"

Mary glanced at Joseph as the old tzaddik lifted his gaze to the heavens. "As you promised, ADONAI, I have seen the Savior you have given to all people. He is a light to reveal God to the nations, and he is the glory of your people Isra'el!"

No sooner had the words left the tzaddik's mouth than an aging woman walked forward. Mary recognized her immediately—Anna, she was called, the daughter of Phanuel. The old prophetess had been a fixture in the Court of the Women for as long as Mary could remember. She did nothing but pray and worship God, day and night, fasting and pleading with ADONAI for the salvation of Isra'el.

Mary listened with amazement as Anna joined the rabbi in praise to the Lord God. "You have spoken truly, Simeon," she cried, her eyes sinking into nets of wrinkles as she smiled. "'Give thanks to ADONAI, for he is good, and his grace continues forever.' This child is the promised King who will deliver Jerusalem."

Mary stood beside Joseph, her heart brimming with feelings too sacred for words, as the righteous tzaddik and the aging prophetess lifted their hands and thanked God for the great things her tiny son would accomplish.

One thought, however, struck Mary on the journey back to Bethlehem. Before they left the Temple, Simeon had looked directly at her and delivered a dire warning.

Why hadn't he included Joseph?

chapter thirty-three

Restless and irritable, Herod shifted on his bed and tossed a bruised grape over his shoulder. Nothing had tasted good today—not his fruit, not his meat, not even the bread he loved.

He bawled for Tero, who finally came running from his own bed-chamber, an urgent question in his eyes. "Is something wrong, Excellency?"

"I cannot sleep." Herod spat the words, then glared at Antipas, who had come in behind Tero. "It has been six weeks, but they have not returned nor have they sent word."

"Who?" Tero asked.

"Don't be impertinent. The magi! They have had plenty of time to find this child, and yet they tell me nothing."

Antipas lifted his hands in a gesture of calm. "Father—," he began.

But Herod would not be patronized. "Do *not* tell me they may yet return! If they were still in the area, we would know it!" He turned his gaze toward the window that opened to a view of the torchlit eastern gates. "Those magi will not be back."

Herod reached for another bunch of grapes and plucked one from the stem. He chewed the fruit, then cocked a brow at Tero. "Is it true that a group of shepherds has been talking about a child born in Bethlehem?"

Tero and Antipas glanced at each other before Tero dipped his head in an abrupt bow. "They are only shepherds, Your Excellency.

They babble about David and stars and angels and miracles—incredible things they imagine in their boredom."

"Perhaps I need to hear from babblers—since my counselor and son have no answers for me." Herod spat the seeds over the edge of his couch, then popped another grape into his mouth. "When," he said, the word rolling around the fruit on his tongue, "did the magi say this child was born?"

Antipas brought his hands together. "They did not know, Father."

"Then how long did they travel?" Herod spat again and leaned forward to drive his point home. "How long have they known about this mysterious star?"

Again, Tero and Antipas looked at one another.

Tero nodded. "Two years, Excellency. They have been watching the star two years."

Herod slammed his hand upon the fruit platter, launching grapes, plums, and dates over the carpets. "Thank you, Tero, for confirming my memory." He drew a long, quivering breath, mastering the passion that drove him. "Now, Counselor. What if my soldiers were to go to this Bethlehem village and find every young child in the area? Every male child under two years of age." He searched his counselor's face. "What would happen to the Hebrews' Messiah then?"

Tero closed his eyes. "Are those the king's wishes?"

"Indeed." Herod leaned back on his elbow. "If a young king has been born in Bethlehem, let him also die there. Tonight." He picked up the solitary grape remaining on the tray, tossed it into his mouth, and grinned at Antipas. "The magi came from the East to honor the Messiah's birth—let us see if the heavens are as eager to commemorate his death."

Antipas gave his father a crooked smile, but Tero bowed and backed out of the room.

Before ordering Herod's captain to ride out, Tero took a few deep breaths to reinforce the frayed fabric of his courage. He had implemented Herod's bloody orders before, but never had he been forced to command the murder of babies.

He shuddered as the image of a sleeping town rose in his mind. This would be a nasty business. Tearing infants from their mother's arms, running a sword through tiny bodies . . .

He glanced at the king's men, who had been pulled from their barracks to saddle their horses in the moonlight. Several of the beasts whickered, unable to understand why they had been led from their warm stalls in the dead of night.

Why? Because the king felt threatened. By a baby.

Yet Herod had killed his own sons for less pressing reasons. He had murdered his wife, whom he worshipped. And what did he feel for Hebrew babies?

Nothing at all.

So this would be a bloody business indeed.

Stretched out on his straw pallet, Joseph whispered a prayer of gratitude for ADONAI's provision. He had reported to the officials; he had registered his name and Mary's on the tax rolls; he had done all that Roman law required of him. He had also circumcised and redeemed his son, fulfilling the law of ADONAI.

Tomorrow he would see if Mary felt strong enough to begin the long journey back to Nazareth. They would proceed slowly, for this time Mary would walk behind him with the baby. The donkey would be loaded with provisions for them, the beast, and the baby, as well as the gifts of the wise men.

Joseph resisted sleep long enough to check on his wife and the infant dozing next to her, then lowered his head to his hands and readied himself for slumber. He had done what God called him to do—he had taken Mary as his wife without shaming her, he had seen her safely to Bethlehem, and by some miracle of grace, he had helped deliver the Son of God. What other man had been called to such tasks?

Now he could return to Nazareth and get back to work. Mary

would be his wife in every way. They would have other children. They would raise their family to respect ADONAI. And HaShem, blessed be his name, would somehow use this little Jesus to usher in the Kingdom of God. . . .

Joseph drowsed for a while on the edge of sleep, then opened his eyes. A vaguely familiar voice spoke in the gloom, urging him to wakefulness with quiet intensity.

Joseph reached for his wife. "Mary," he whispered, not wanting to wake Thomas and his family. "You must wake."

Her eyes sprang open, as if she'd been slapped from sleep. "Is something wrong with the baby?"

"Gather our things and meet me in the stable with the baby. Hurry."

Joseph lingered long enough for her to read the seriousness in his countenance; then he rose and strode toward the stable, where the donkey waited.

In the moonlit fields outside Bethlehem, Ozni plucked a piece of straw from his mouth and stared as a thundering column of mounted soldiers approached the sleeping city. Instinctively he reached for his favorite lamb, holding her close as the soldiers churned the dust on the road and sent it boiling into the night.

Mary walked into the stable with a brisk step, the baby in a sling and their meager belongings in a leather satchel.

Joseph noticed, however, that she had brought no food. He fastened the last waterskin on the donkey, tightened the girth strap, and rested his arms on the animal's back. "No bread or cheese?"

A clap of thunder rattled in the distance as Mary shook her head. "I could not take Deborah's food. Perhaps we can buy something on the way." She lifted a brow. "Perhaps you can tell me why we're sneaking out like a family of thieves."

Joseph took the bag from her, tied it onto the saddle, then tugged on the animal's bridle. "We should go."

"Now?" Honest alarm crossed Mary's face. "I wanted to wake Thomas and Deborah. I need to thank them for their hospitality."

"Mary—" Joseph gentled his tone—"you have thanked them every day for six weeks. They know you are appreciative."

When she bit her lip and cast a longing look toward the house, he knew he'd have to tell her the truth.

"I had a dream," he said, leading the donkey into the alley. "An angel of ADONAI told me to get up and flee to Egypt with you and the baby. Herod is going to try to kill the child."

A tremor rippled across Mary's shoulders as she touched her sleeping son's head.

"And so," Joseph said, settling their belongings more evenly on the donkey's blanket, "we will trust ADONAI to bless Thomas and his wife. As for us, we will obey."

He knew she would not protest again.

Ozni walked slowly through the narrow street, mingling among the shadows as screams shattered the quiet night. Herod's soldiers had invaded every house, battering their way past doors and pulling men, women, and children into a thundering storm.

As rain bounced off rooftops and thunder drowned out passionate protests, Herod's soldiers examined family members with hard, passionless eyes. While children cried in confusion and parents wailed in grief, the soldiers gathered all babies younger than two years and carried them to a man who stood at the ancient town center.

Ozni stood across from the well and blinked as the screaming intensified and the circle of soldiers expanded. Herod's mercenaries dropped screaming babies, their arms outstretched, to the cobbled pavement while powerless fathers wrestled against armed men who held them in stalwart grips.

When the company of soldiers had visited every house, every inn, and every shelter outside the village walls, more than forty infants and toddlers had been brought to the captain of Herod's guard. Their parents had followed as inevitably as the day follows the sun, and most of the mothers' wailing subsided as the parents waited to see what the king's man would do.

As black rain poured from the night sky, the captain barked a question to the last guard, a young man who carried a dark-haired infant by his swaddling clothes.

"That's it," the soldier answered, depositing the baby with the others. "The last one."

The captain nodded to one of his men, who drew his sword. Ozni watched, gripping his lamb, as the swordsman moved from one child to the next, ripping off tiny robes and unwinding the swaddling of newborns. Some of the children he dropped back to the ground unharmed, but others he handed to another guard, who held the screaming infants aloft while the swordsman struck.

Ozni closed his eyes against the carnage, his heart squeezed so tight he could barely draw breath. Some of the mothers fainted; others dissolved into whimpering heaps as their husbands cursed and ranted, helpless against the flashing blade of Herod's executioner.

The aged rabbi stood with his keening daughter, his pale face streaming with rain and tears. "This is what the Lord says," he cried, his voice breaking. "'A cry of anguish is heard in Ramah—mourning and weeping unrestrained. Rachel weeps for her children, refusing to be comforted—for her children are dead.'"

Swallowing the sob that rose in his throat, Ozni lifted his gaze to the dissolving sky, where only a few nights before, the star of hope had lit the way for outcasts and magi to find the child of peace.

Had that child been caught in Herod's trap?

chapter thirty-four

A rising wind whooshed past Mary, lifting her veil and whipping her tunic tight around her legs. She adjusted the sling until the baby's weight was distributed more evenly across her neck and back, then hurried to catch up to her husband.

Behind them, in the sky over Bethlehem, arteries of lightning pulsed in the clouds, but the road that would lead them south to Egypt remained clear.

Her father had been wise to choose Joseph for her husband. She had known so little in the days before her betrothal; she had been a child herself. But now . . . now she had seen and heard much.

Her mind drifted back to Simeon, the old tzaddik at the Temple. From scores of women he had picked her out and come to her, his arms open for the baby. Without a word of explanation, he had known who Jesus was, who *she* was.

He had recognized the hope of the world.

And then Simeon had spoken not only about Jesus, but about her. His dark eyes had shimmered with mystery when he lowered his gaze to hers and said, "This child will be rejected by many in Isra'el, and it will be their undoing. But he will be the greatest joy to many others. Thus, the deepest thoughts of many hearts will be revealed. And a sword will pierce your very soul."

The words had rung with familiarity. She had no idea what the old tzaddik meant or why he did not warn Joseph, but she did not doubt him. ADONAI had been kind to warn her of the difficulties ahead; even now the Almighty One was helping them protect this vulnerable Son of God.

So . . . if God had ordained a sword to pierce her soul, she would accept it. Even welcome it, as she had welcomed the agony of childbirth. For out of the greatest pain came the greatest joy, along with strength to face the next trial.

Mary lifted her gaze and fastened it to the place where Joseph's head met his strong shoulders.

The Master of the Universe had sent her a good man. He'd seen fit to entrust them with the task of raising the Light of the World, so he would give them the courage to face the darkness. Thus far in ADONAI's service, Mary had known fear, scorn, pain, and hunger. But those hardships could not compare to the joy of knowing that God saw her, a willing vessel, and chose to fill her with light. With love. With hope.

Not only for her but for all mankind.

epilogue

After a bloody reign of thirty-seven years, Herod the Great died in his palace at Jericho, murderous until the end. Only five days before he succumbed to a long and painful illness, Herod executed his son Antipater. Worried that his own death would cause celebration throughout his kingdom, Herod ordered all the noblemen of Israel brought to Jericho and shut up in the Hippodrome so they could be executed immediately after he died. Fortunately, Salome, the sister to whom he gave this nefarious order, had the good sense to release the noblemen, thus increasing the celebration in Israel and thwarting Herod's final wishes.

After Herod the Great's death, Rome divided his kingdom among his sons Archelaus, Antipas, and Philip, though Archelaus's kingdom soon fell under the jurisdiction of Roman procurators.

Mary, Joseph, and Jesus remained in Egypt until an angel again appeared to Joseph in a dream and told him it was safe to return to Israel (Matthew 2:13-15). Joseph went immediately to Judea, but upon hearing that Herod's son Archelaus ruled that region, he took his small family to Galilee . . . and home to Nazareth. This fulfilled what the prophets had said about the Messiah—that he would be called out of Egypt (Hosea 11:1) and that he would be called a Nazarene. (*Nazarene* comes from the Hebrew word *netzer*, meaning "branch," a term often applied by the prophets. See Isaiah 4:2, 11:1; Jeremiah 23:5, 33:15; Zechariah 3:8, 6:12-13).

Zechariah and Elizabeth's son, John, became a prophet and paved the way for the Messiah. He would later baptize Jesus in the Jordan River. After John was imprisoned and beheaded by Herod Antipas, Jesus told his followers, "I assure you, of all who have ever lived, none is greater than John the Baptist" (Matthew 11:11).

John was never "great" in an earthly sense, for he lived alone in the desert, wore animal skins, and ate locusts and wild honey, but no man was more humble or committed to his God-ordained task (Matthew 3:3-4; Mark 1:6).

Mary and Joseph had other children, providing Jesus with several half sisters and half brothers named James, Joseph, Simon, and Judas. Apparently Jesus' siblings doubted his claims at the beginning of his ministry (John 7:5), but after Jesus' death and resurrection, James became the leader of the church at Jerusalem, and his other brothers also believed (Acts 1:14).

Mary, the young mother who believed despite dangerous uncertainties, witnessed Jesus' earthly ministry and was present at his crucifixion (Matthew 27:55-56). At that moment, surely she knew what Simeon meant when he predicted that a sword would pierce her soul. But though she suffered things we can't imagine, she knew of her son's resurrection and was among those praying and waiting for the advent of the Holy Spirit on Pentecost (Acts 1:14).

Joseph, the devout man who loved Mary enough not to shame her, served as Jesus' adoptive father for many years. He was present when twelve-year-old Jesus lingered at the Temple in Jerusalem (Luke 2:41-51), but Joseph was not on the scene when Jesus began his ministry at age thirty.

Though Joseph the quiet carpenter is absent for much of the gospel story, his influence undoubtedly helped shape the human life of the one who was known as the carpenter from Nazareth, the adopted son of Joseph, and Jesus, the Son of God.

about the author

Christy-Award winner Angela Hunt writes books for readers who have learned to expect the unexpected. With over 3 million copies of her books sold worldwide, she is the best-selling author of *The Tale of Three Trees*, *The Note*, *Unspoken*, and more than 100 other titles.

She and her youth pastor husband make their home in Florida with mastiffs. One of their dogs was featured on *Live with Regis and Kelly* as the second-largest canine in America.

Readers may visit her Web site at www.angelahuntbooks.com.

about the screenwriter

Mike Rich's screenwriting breakthrough occurred in 1998 when his script for *Finding Forrester* was honored by the Academy of Motion Picture Arts and Sciences Nicholl Fellowship competition. He followed the release of that film with his screenplays for *The Rookie* and *Radio*. Consistently attracted to strong, character-driven pieces, Rich recently completed work on his adaptation of James Swanson's best seller *Manhunt*, a historical look at the search for Lincoln assassin John Wilkes Booth

discussion questions

1. Compare and contrast the film *The Nativity Story* with the novel. What advantages does film have over the printed page? What advantages does the printed page have over film?

2. What did you learn about life in first-century Judea from viewing the film or reading the novel?

3. Film relies on dialogue and visual images to tell a story; a novel must create dialogue and images with words. Did you find the novel as effective as the film in creating the mood and setting of the story? Was the film as effective as the novel in sharing facts of historical and cultural significance?

4. What are some of the major themes of the story?

5. Would you recommend the film and/or the novel to people who do not consider themselves Christians? What effect do you think it might have on them?

6. What did you learn about Elizabeth and Zechariah that you had not considered before?

7. Why do you suppose Herod the Great was so jealous of his position?

8. What did you think about the magi? Were they true spiritual seekers or merely curious astronomers? How do you suppose the journey to Judea changed them?

9. In Mary's hymn of praise, known as the *Magnificat*, she says, "Oh, how I praise the Lord. How I rejoice in God my Savior!" What does this tell us about Mary's view of herself?

10. Were you surprised to read of Mary's wish for other children? Did you know Jesus had half brothers and sisters? (His brothers' names are listed in Matthew 13:55-56 and Mark 6:3).

11. Is there anything in Mary's life to which you can personally relate? How is she like you? How is she different?

12. What do you think Mary saw as her biggest challenge? How did God prepare her for the task of mothering the Son of God?

an interview with
angela hunt

Q: Were you at all nervous about attempting to portray such a significant story?

AH: I'd use the word *excited.* I had Mike Rich's excellent screenplay to use as a basis for the novel, plus I had the Scriptures and dozens of reference books. I wanted to document as much as possible and create a story based on what we know about these historical characters who lived in first-century Judea.

Q: Of all the women in Judea, why do you think God chose Mary to give birth to the Savior of the world?

AH: While I can't presume to know the mind of God, I realized something while I was working on the scenes in which Mary traveled to see Elizabeth. In my first draft, I had Mary thinking the sort of thoughts *I'd* think if I were her: *Am I delusional? Was I hallucinating when I saw the angel? If Elizabeth really is pregnant, I'll know I didn't dream that encounter in the olive grove.*

I had to strike all those thoughts when I studied Elizabeth's response to Mary. Luke 1:45 tells us that when she saw her young cousin, Elizabeth said, "You are blessed, because *you believed that the Lord would do what he said*" (emphasis added).

While I'm sure Galilee was filled with virtuous young virgins who loved and followed ADONAI, I'm not sure there were many who had Mary's pure faith. She went to see Elizabeth not to test the angel's word but fully and happily expecting to find her aging cousin six months pregnant.

Mary provides a stark contrast with Zechariah—the priest doubted the angel, but the young girl accepted Gabriel's word with unquestioning faith and obedience.

Q: Your depiction of the magi might lead someone to think you are endorsing astrology. Are you?

AH: Absolutely not. Scripture expressly forbids the worship of the sun, moon, or stars (Deuteronomy 4:19). We can certainly study the stars as an astronomer might, but we are not to place our faith in them or believe they hold the key to our future.

The magi from the East (probably Persia or Babylonia, but no one knows exactly where they came from or how many magi made the journey) had more in common with the Jews' religion than any other nation. Though they did not worship Jehovah, they believed in one true God, they did not worship idols, and they considered light the best symbol of God. They had heard of the Hebrews; they were probably familiar with Daniel, the great rab-mag who had interpreted puzzling dreams while in captivity in Babylon; and they recognized that the order and design of the universe demanded a Creator.

In *History of the Christian Church*, Philip and David Schaff propose that God "condescended to the astrological faith of the Magi, and probably made also an internal revelation to them before, as well as after the appearance of the star."*

_____

*Philip Schaff and David Schley Schaff, *History of the Christian Church* (Oak Harbor, WA: Logos Research Systems, Inc., 1997).

While several theories attempt to explain the star of Bethlehem, Mike Rich and I chose to use a combination of natural and supernatural methods. The star was a heavenly body or a conjunction of heavenly bodies, but as the magi's caravan approached Bethlehem, the star moved in an explicit way that both surprised and delighted the magi (Matthew 2:9-10). Since the star actually moved and stood over the house where the child was, I envisioned it beaming a light rather like the pillar of fire that led the Israelites through the wilderness. This was definitely a supernatural effect.

As we consider the magi, let's not forget that *all* of creation testifies to God's creative power:

> *The heavens tell of the glory of God.*
> *The skies display his marvelous craftsmanship.*
> *Day after day they continue to speak; night after night they*
>   *make him known.*
> *They speak without a sound or a word: their voice is silent*
>   *in the skies;*
> *yet their message has gone out to all the earth,*
> *and their words to all the world.*   PSALM 19:1-4

If the heavens do all of the above . . . why shouldn't God send a star to announce his Son's birth?

Q: Speaking of the magi, *when* did they find Mary, Joseph, and the baby? The film and novel depict them arriving on the night of Christ's birth, but some experts say it may have taken them as long as two years to find Jesus.

AH: No one knows exactly when the magi arrived. If you accept that the Bethlehem star might have been a conjunction of stars the magi would have recognized and anticipated, it's possible they arrived very soon after the baby's birth.

Others have theorized that the magi didn't see the star until after Jesus' arrival, so they took as long as two years to make their way to Bethlehem. Scripture does say they found Jesus in a house, not a stable, though the stable might have been attached to a house.

The Greek word for the Christ child in Luke 2:16, when the shepherds found him, is *brephos*, the word for "infant;" the word for the Christ child in Matthew 2:9, when the magi arrived, is *padion*, a word usually reserved for a child of about eighteen months. It is hard to imagine, though, why Mary and Joseph would have lingered in Bethlehem for eighteen months.

Q: So when did Herod slaughter the children of Bethlehem?

AH: For the novel, I wanted to include the biblical scenes of Mary's purification in the Temple, a rite that would have taken place forty days after her baby's birth. I believe Herod's bloody assault could not have occurred until some time after Mary and Joseph's visit to Jerusalem.

Q: One more thing—I was a little confused by the terms *rabbi*, *priest*, *Levites*, and *tzaddik*. Aren't they all the same thing?

AH: No. The Levites, descended from the tribe of Levi, were set apart to serve in the Temple. Each man had to serve a set "course," or term, and fulfill his duty in Jerusalem.

The descendants of Aaron, the *cohanim*, were a subgroup of Levites who served as priests. The priests offered sacrifices and participated in holy rituals; the other Levites served as singers, musicians, worship leaders, and support personnel. All priests were Levites, but not all Levites were priests.

A rabbi is a person qualified to teach about Jewish law. The teacher in a village synagogue would be a rabbi. A rabbi is not necessarily a priest, for a priest, or *cohen*, must be a descendant of Aaron. A priest can be a rabbi, but not all rabbis are priests.

The word *tzaddik* literally means "righteous one." Like Simeon, this could be a priest or rabbi who has great spiritual wisdom or power.

I hope you enjoyed reading the story as much as I did writing it!

references

Achtemeier, Paul J. *Harper's Bible Dictionary.* San Francisco: Harper & Row, 1985.

Bell, Albert A. *Exploring the New Testament World.* Nashville: Thomas Nelson Publishers, 1998.

Blomberg, Craig. *The New American Commentary.* Nashville: Broadman & Holman Publishers, 2001, c1992.

Cargal, Timothy B. *So That's Why! Bible.* Nashville: Thomas Nelson Publishers, 2001.

Courson, Jon. *Jon Courson's Application Commentary.* Nashville: Thomas Nelson Publishers, 2003.

Criswell Center for Biblical Studies. *Believer's Study Bible.* Nashville: Thomas Nelson, 1997.

du Toit, A.B. *The New Testament Milieu.* Halfway House: Orion, 1998.

Easton, M.G. *Easton's Bible Dictionary.* Oak Harbor, WA: Logos Research Systems, Inc., 1996, c1897.

Edersheim, Alfred. *Sketches of Jewish Social Life in the Days of Christ.* Bellingham, WA: Logos Research Systems, Inc., 2003.

Edersheim, Alfred. *The Life and Times of Jesus the Messiah*. Bellingham, WA: Logos Research Systems, Inc., 1896, 2003.

Edersheim, Alfred. *The Temple, Its Ministry and Services as They were at the Time of Jesus Christ*. Bellingham, WA: Logos Research Systems, Inc., 2003.

Elwell, Walter A. and Philip Wesley Comfort. *Tyndale Bible Dictionary*. Wheaton, IL: Tyndale House Publishers, 2001.

Freedman, David Noel. *The Anchor Bible Dictionary*. New York: Doubleday, 1996, c1992.

Freeman, James M. and Harold J. Chadwick. *Manners & Customs of the Bible*. North Brunswick, NJ: Bridge-Logos Publishers, 1998.

Hagee, John. *His Glory Revealed*. Nashville: Thomas Nelson Publishers, 1999.

Isachar, Hanan. *Images of the Holy Land*. Oak Harbor, WA: Logos Research Systems, 1997.

Jamieson, Robert, A. R. Fausset, et al. *A Commentary, Critical and Explanatory, on the Old and New Testaments: Critical and Explanatory Commentary*. Oak Harbor, WA: Logos Research Systems, Inc., 1997.

Jenkins, Simon. *Nelson's 3-D Bible Mapbook*. Nashville: Thomas Nelson Publishers, 1997, c1985.

Kaiser, Walter C. *Hard Sayings of the Bible*. Downers Grove, IL: InterVarsity Press, 1997, c1996.

Keener, Craig S. and InterVarsity Press. *The IVP Bible Background Commentary: New Testament*. Downers Grove, IL: InterVarsity Press, 1993.

Keil, Carl Friedrich and Franz Delitzsch. *Commentary on the Old Testament*. Peabody, MA: Hendrickson, 2002.

Keppie, Lawrence. *The Making of the Roman Army: From Republic to Empire.* Norman, OK: University of Oklahoma Press, 1998.

Kibbey, Hal. "Star of Bethlehem May Have Been Planets Jupiter, Venus." Indiana University: Office of Communications and Marketing, no date given. http://newsinfo.iu.edu/OCM/packages/bethstar.html.

Lagass, Paul and Columbia University. *The Columbia Encyclopedia,* 6th ed. New York, Detroit: Columbia University Press, 2000.

MacArthur, John. *God in the Manger: The Miraculous Birth of Christ.* Nashville: W Pub. Group, 2001.

MacDonald, William and Arthur Farstad. *Believer's Bible Commentary: Old and New Testaments.* Nashville: Thomas Nelson Publishers, 1997, c1995.

Malina, Bruce and Stephan Joubert. *A Time Travel to the World of Jesus.* Halfway House: Orion, 1997, c1996.

McGarvey, John William. *The Four-Fold Gospel.* Oak Harbor, WA: Logos Research Systems, Inc., 1999.

McGee, J. Vernon. *Thru the Bible Commentary, Based on the Thru the Bible Radio Program.* Nashville: Thomas Nelson Publishers, 1997, c1981.

Mills, M.S. *The Life of Christ: A Study Guide to the Gospel Record,* Three volumes: 1. *The Advent of Jesus* 2. *The Beginning of the Gospel* 3. *Jesus presents Himself to Israel.* Dallas: 3E Ministries, 1999.

Negev, Avraham. *The Archaeological Encyclopedia of the Holy Land,* 3rd ed. New York: Prentice Hall Press, 1996, c1990.

Newman, Robert C. "The Star of Bethlehem: A Natural-Supernatural Hybrid?" Biblical Theological Seminary, Interdisciplinary Biblical Research Institute, 2001, http://www.ibri.org/Papers/StarofBethlehem/75starbethlehem.htm.

Packer, J.I., Merrill Chapin Tenney, and William White. *Nelson's Illustrated Manners and Customs of the Bible.* Nashville: Thomas Nelson Publishers, 1997, c1995.

Radmacher, Earl D., Ronald Barclay Allen, and H. Wayne House. *The Nelson Study Bible: New King James Version.* Nashville: Thomas Nelson Publishers, 1997.

Radmacher, Earl D., Ronald Barclay Allen, and H. Wayne House. *Nelson's New Illustrated Bible Commentary.* Nashville: Thomas Nelson Publishers, 1999.

Richards, Larry and Lawrence O Richards. *The Teacher's Commentary.* Wheaton, IL: Victor Books, 1987.

Richards, Sue Poorman and Larry Richards. *Every Woman in the Bible.* Nashville: Thomas Nelson Publishers, 1999.

Schaff, Philip and David Schley Schaff. *History of the Christian Church.* Oak Harbor, WA: Logos Research Systems, Inc., 1997.

Smith, William. *Smith's Bible Dictionary.* Nashville: Thomas Nelson Publishers, 1997.

Stern, David H. *Jewish New Testament Commentary: A Companion Volume to the Jewish New Testament.* Clarksville, MD: Jewish New Testament Publications, 1996, c1992.

Swindoll, Charles R. and Roy B. Zuck. *Understanding Christian Theology.* Nashville: Thomas Nelson Publishers, 2003.

Thomas Nelson Publishers, *Nelson's Quick Reference Topical Bible Index.* Nashville: Thomas Nelson Publishers, 1995.

Thomas Nelson Publishers. *The Ultimate A to Z Resource Fully Illustrated.* Nashville: Thomas Nelson Publishers, 2001.

Unterman, Alan. *Dictionary of Jewish Lore & Legend.* New York: Thames and Hudson Ltd., 1991.

Vos, Howard Frederic. *Nelson's New Illustrated Bible Manners &*
Customs: How the People of the Bible Really Lived. Nashville:
Thomas Nelson Publishers, 1999.

Willmington, H. L. *Willmington's Bible Handbook.* Wheaton, IL:
Tyndale House Publishers, 1997.

Wood, D. R. W. and I. Howard Marshall. *New Bible Dictionary.*
Downers Grove: InterVarsity Press, 1996, c1982, c1962.

Youngblood, F., F. F. Bruce, R. K. Harrison, and Thomas Nelson
Publishers. *Nelson's New Illustrated Bible Dictionary.* Nashville:
Thomas Nelson Publishers, 1995.

Zuck, Roy B. and Dallas Theological Seminary. *The Bible Knowledge*
Commentary: An Exposition of the Scriptures. Wheaton, IL:
Victor Books, 1983-c1985.

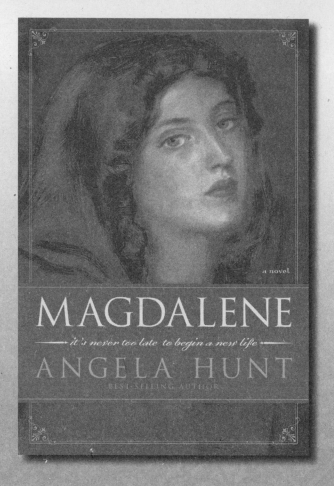

a novel

MAGDALENE

it's never too late to begin a new life

ANGELA HUNT

BEST-SELLING AUTHOR

The controversial woman with a past only one man could forgive.
A true love story that changed the face of history.

For more information visit:

www.tyndalefiction.com

www.angelahuntbooks.com

it's never too late to begin a new life

OTHER NOVELS BY
ANGELA HUNT

HISTORICAL:
Magdalene
The Shadow Women
The Silver Sword
The Golden Cross
The Velvet Shadow
The Emerald Isle
Dreamers
Brothers
Journey

CONTEMPORARY:
The Novelist
A Time to Mend
Unspoken
The Truth Teller
The Awakening
The Debt
The Canopy
The Pearl
The Justice
The Note
The Immortal

For a complete listing, visit
www.angelahuntbooks.com

Other Nativity books
from Tyndale

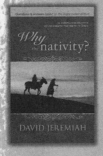